HIS SUBMISSIVE

Boston Doms - Book Two

JANE HENRY
MAISY ARCHER

Published by Blushing Books
An Imprint of
ABCD Graphics and Design, Inc.
A Virginia Corporation
977 Seminole Trail #233
Charlottesville, VA 22901

©2019
All rights reserved.

No part of the book may be reproduced or transmitted in any form or by any means, electronic or mechanical, including photocopying, recording, or by any information storage and retrieval system, without permission in writing from the publisher. The trademark Blushing Books is pending in the US Patent and Trademark Office.

Jane Henry and Maisy Archer
His Submissive

EBook ISBN: 978-1-68259-691-3
Print ISBN: 978-1-64563-160-6
v1

Cover Art by ABCD Graphics & Design
This book contains fantasy themes appropriate for mature readers only. Nothing in this book should be interpreted as Blushing Books' or the author's advocating any non-consensual sexual activity.

Chapter 1

Hillary heaved open the steel fire door that led from the kitchen to the alley behind the restaurant, grateful that the noise from the party masked the protesting squeal of the hinges.

She *loved* her sister and soon-to-be brother-in-law, she truly did, and she was *thrilled* to celebrate their engagement with the rest of their family and friends. After all, Heidi and her fiancé, Dominic Angelico, had been through a lot over the past few months, and no one knew Heidi deserved happiness as well as Hillary did. But after two hours of watching Heidi and Dom wrapped around each other, and their friend Paul and his boyfriend John making eyes at one another, and *certain other people* flirting with *every woman in the room but her*, Hillary needed to escape. The cloying scent of romance was thick in the air, and it was giving her a headache.

She stepped out into the humid August night, sucked in a deep, calming breath of air... and immediately wrinkled her nose. *Ah, the smell of garbage in summer,* she thought with a laugh. *A much more appropriate fragrance for my mood.*

She propped the door open with practiced ease, using the

heavy bucket that was kept just inside the door for that very purpose, and leaned her back against the rough brick wall of the building. Though she'd kept company with Nicole and the other waitresses and line cooks a million times as they took their smoke breaks back here, the alley behind *Cara* still felt sinister in the darkness. From the hulking shadows of the dumpsters and parked cars, she could hear the scratching and scrabbling of little creatures she preferred not to think about... and who knew what other, *human* dangers were hiding out there?

Hillary shivered and edged a few inches closer to the door.

She'd only wanted to experience the kind of pleasure she'd read about—the kind she wanted to *write* about, the kind that came from submitting yourself completely to someone else's control. But she'd been a college senior, and that wasn't exactly the kind of thing you could mention to a guy at a fraternity mixer. So she'd found a willing dominant online last April.

Marauder.

The first in a string of poor decisions where her heart was concerned.

Marauder had made all kinds of dark promises in his emails—restraints and punishments, things so taboo that she'd blushed like a middle-schooler. She'd naively assumed that it was all part of the game, that the romance would come later.

Dumb, dumb, dumb.

Real life was nothing like a romance novel.

The smooth, unrelenting steel of the bench beneath her back. Her wrists and ankles bound with hard metal cuffs that cut off her circulation and chafed when she struggled. The gag that almost choked her. The overpowering fear, until Matteo broke down the door and...

No.

The shit that went down at Club Black Box was *over* and it would *never* happen again.

You are a different person now, she reminded herself.

Hillary blew out a breath and ran a hand through her cap of short hair, trying unsuccessfully to tuck one of the longer front strands behind her ear. *Almost, but not quite.*

One of the first things she'd done after graduating and moving down to Boston in May was to find a hair dresser who'd transformed her shoulder-length auburn hair into a modified blond pixie-cut, liberally streaked with blue and purple. It had sounded so badass, so edgy, so perfect for starting a new chapter in her life.

Her sister had warned her that she'd regret it—that the novelty would fade and she'd be annoyed with how long it took to grow out.

And it turned out that Heidi had been partially right—the cut had proved annoying *and* regrettable. Though not for the reasons Heidi had imagined.

"Hey, Tinker Bell," mocked a deep, smooth voice from the kitchen. "Whatcha doin' out there?"

Ugh! That *name!* Hillary whirled around, ready to murder the person speaking it... but it wasn't the Angelico brother she'd been expecting, so instead she rolled her eyes.

"You have a death wish tonight, Tony?" she asked sweetly, folding her arms over her chest as she regarded Dom's youngest brother Tony, the owner of *Cara*.

In the light spilling through the doorway, she could see that his expensive suit was creased, his brown hair was rumpled, his hazel eyes were glassy and he carried a beer bottle in each hand.

Looked like *someone* had been enjoying the party.

Tony snickered like what she'd said was extremely funny. "No more than usual. And where's the gratitude? Is that any way to talk to your boss?"

Hillary rolled her eyes again and fought a smile. It was true that Tony had offered her a part-time waitress gig at *Cara* as soon as she'd moved to town. And with its prime North End location and influx of summer tourists, the tips allowed her to work relatively few hours each week, making it the perfect job for a writer struggling to finish her first novel. But although Tony owned the restaurant, he hardly ever acted like her boss. Instead, it was the restaurant manager, pretty, take-charge Tessa Damon, who mostly ran the business these days, leaving Tony free to run the kitchen, the way he preferred.

Tony smiled widely, amused by her attitude. The white flash of his teeth and an adorable dimple softened the hard lines of his face, and she wondered for the umpteenth time why the hell it couldn't be *this* Angelico who filled her every thought. Tony was tall, like both of his brothers, but broader and huskier. He was open and friendly, where Dom was reserved. And Tony was sweet and sympathetic, unlike the high-handed, alpha-male, crazy-making, unbelievably sexy force of nature that was Dom's twin brother, Matteo.

"Peace offering," Tony told her, handing her one of the beers he carried and sitting down heavily on the bucket in front of the door.

"Hmm," Hillary murmured noncommittally, taking a deep pull of the beer. Sam Adams, her favorite. A decent peace offering. Still… "You know I don't answer to that name. *Ever*."

He shrugged. "It's catchy. And for what it's worth, I'm pretty sure Matteo didn't intend to piss you off when he came up with it," he told her, his eyes dancing. "How was he supposed to know you had such a deep hatred of pixies?"

Hillary gritted her teeth. She had nothing against pixies, per se. She *did* have something against the idiot who'd taken one look at her badass haircut and vertically-challenged stature and immediately thought of an animated fairy rather than a strong, mature, sexy woman.

"Well if it were unintentional, you'd think he'd have gotten a clue the first twelve thousand times I told him not to call me that!" she groused.

"Oh, I just said he didn't intend to piss you off *at first*," Tony said cheerfully, taking another swig from his bottle. "But *now* he definitely does it just to piss you off."

Hillary raised one eyebrow and looked at Tony, who smiled back at her with mock innocence. But then he grew serious.

"Is he why you're out here?"

Hillary stiffened. "Who? Matteo?" she scoffed. "No. Of course not. I've hardly spoken to him tonight. I just needed fresh air."

It was bad enough that Matteo already knew how she felt about him, thanks to her stupid decision to bare her soul to him one night a couple of weeks ago. If Tony or anyone else suspected that she had one-sided feelings for Matteo, the humiliation might kill her.

It was Tony's turn to raise an eyebrow. "Don't play dumb, Hillie. I saw Matteo doing his thing in there, flirting with your cousin Sara *and* Heidi's friend Marlene. And then I saw you come out here."

Shit. She'd tried to be so careful. Hillary swallowed hard and scrambled for an explanation.

"Because I know it must drive you crazy," he continued. "You know... as a feminist."

What?

Oh.

Right. Yes. It bothered her as a *feminist*. Clearly.

She almost sighed in relief.

"If it helps, from what I hear it's a genetic thing. They say our dad was the same way before he got married. Matt can't help but flirt with every woman over eighteen and under fifty..." He paused to consider. "Maybe sixty," he amended, then continued with a shrug. "He doesn't mean anything by it."

She nodded. This was true—flirting was the only way that Matteo related to women, whether it was the grandmotherly lady who rolled gnocchi in Tony's kitchen once a week, or the pretty teenage cashier at the corner store, or Hillary's own middle-aged, hippy mother.

"Except Heidi," she reminded him. "And, well…me."

Tony shrugged and nodded. "Well, *yeah*. Except you two. Since you're family."

Right. Yes. *Family*. Brother- and sister-in-law.

Except that her feelings toward Matteo hadn't ever been sisterly, not from the moment he'd broken down the door at Club Black Box and saved her from that asshole, taken her back to his apartment, listened to her hesitant, stammering confessions about wanting to be a submissive, and helped her begin to heal. She wanted him, no holds barred.

And for a brief moment, she had imagined that he felt the same way… before he'd completely shut her down.

She shook her head and changed the subject.

"Anyway, what brings *you* to this scenic spot, Boss Man?" she asked, waving a hand to indicate the nearby trashcans. "Won't Val be looking for you?"

Tony's girlfriend Val rarely let him out of her sight when there were single women around.

He laughed without humor. "Oh, no doubt. She's probably got more bitching to do about the arrangement of the tables or the wines we're serving with dinner. Why do you think I'm out here? You know she won't come through the kitchen. Might ruin her shoes."

Hillary's head went back in surprise. She'd always thought of Val as catty and shallow—just that night, she'd accused Hillary of ruining the 'elegance' of the wedding party pictures with her funky hair and plain blue sheath dress. And she knew Dom worried that Tony would let Val suck him dry financially. But she'd never heard Tony say a word against her until now.

"She bitched so much that you let her run you out of your own restaurant?" she scolded.

Tony leveled such a stern, forbidding look at her that she winced. Jeez, maybe he wasn't *just* sweet and cheerful.

"Sorry, sorry," she backtracked quickly. "I just mean..."

But he sighed and looked away, rubbing the back of his neck.

"No, you're right. I prefer to think of it as a strategic retreat, rather than running away," he said sardonically. "But I guess it's the same thing." He paused a moment before continuing. "Val wants a ring."

Hillary choked on a sip of beer.

"A *what?*"

Tony slumped forward, resting his elbows on his knees.

"An engagement ring. She and I have been dating for over a year now," he said. "And Dom only met Heidi... what, four months ago?"

Hillary scowled. "Yeah, but that's different. When it's *right* like that, you just... *know.*"

Tony nodded. "Yup. *You* know that, and *I* know that, but Val..." He tipped the beer to his lips again, drained the last few drops, and shrugged. "Val wants a ring."

Oh, wow. Val for a sister-in-law?

"Damn," Hillary breathed. "But... You know it's not all about what Val wants, Tony. What about you? What do *you* want?"

But before Tony could answer, a loud burst of laughter made them both turn toward the kitchen.

The first thing Hillary saw was Matteo... And wasn't *that* the story of her life, at least for the past few months? He was always the first thing she noticed, a magnet that drew her eyes the second he walked in the room.

Tall and tan, larger than life, his head thrown back with laughter. And, God, how did he manage to look so elegant, despite the muscles that rippled and flexed beneath his dark grey suit jacket? Her fingers tingled with the need to touch him.

And then she noticed his companion.

Tessa was standing next to him, and she was smiling, too, looking for all the world like an auburn Jessica Rabbit in a tight, strapless pink dress that Hillary didn't have the assets to hold up if her life depended on it.

Is it any wonder Matteo isn't interested in being anything more than your brother? Hillary thought miserably as her stomach churned.

"Seriously, Matt," Tessa chided gently, shaking her head at Matteo in exasperation, even as she smiled. "You're crazy. I don't think—"

But Matteo smiled down at Tessa and draped one muscular arm around Tessa's slim shoulders... her slim *bare* shoulders.

"Honey, do you trust me?" he asked, in that deep, resonant voice that haunted Hillary's dreams. "I'm telling you, Tess, a man like me *knows* when..."

Tony pushed himself to his feet, vibrating with tension, and Matteo's eyes caught the motion, his gaze swinging to the doorway. His eyes widened as he caught sight of Tony and then narrowed when he spied Hillary. Matteo scowled.

"Tony? What are you doing out there?" Matteo demanded.

Tony's jaw worked for a moment before he spoke, and when he did, it was in a low voice, to Hillary.

"I don't think it matters what *I* want, Hill," he told her. Then he chucked his empty beer bottle into the recycling dumpster and walked back inside to stand in front of his brother and Tessa.

"Matt," Tony said, lifting his chin in greeting. Then he folded his arms across his chest. "Miss Damon. I thought you were working tonight."

"I... am," Tessa said in confusion, stepping away from Matteo. "That's why I'm h—"

"Really? That's funny," Tony interrupted, cocking his head to the side, "because the party is out *there*, and you're in *here*."

Hillary saw Tess's eyes narrow.

"But I was just—"

"In the future, Miss Damon, I'd appreciate it if you'd save your personal conversations for after work."

He pushed his way between Tessa and Matteo and stomped over to the small office off to the side of the kitchen, slamming the door behind him.

Tessa looked outraged. She narrowed her eyes at the closed door like she was contemplating violence. But finally she turned and stalked toward the swinging door that led to the front of the restaurant, slapping it open with her palm. She held it open just long enough to turn and look back at Matteo.

"Looks like you were wrong. But thanks anyway, Matt," she said.

Then she spun around, her brown hair flying out behind her, and disappeared through the door.

All the while, Matteo looked extremely pleased with himself. He seemed to be fighting a smile.

"Holy crap! You think this was *funny*?" Hillary exploded. "You are unbelievable! You got your brother all upset, and you got Tessa in trouble with her boss!"

Matteo turned to face her fully, his eyes scanning quickly from her hair, to her dress, to her shoes, and then back up, focusing on the drink in her hand. His smile evaporated and he raised one eyebrow.

"Why, hello, Hillary," he said pointedly. "It's lovely to see you this fine evening."

Hillary rolled her eyes, even as a part of her squirmed at the subtle rebuke. Why did he always seem to turn her into a senseless puddle of goo or a raving shrew?

She leaned back against the doorframe and sipped her beer, glaring at him.

He walked over and leaned against the opposite side of the doorframe, facing her, so close that his folded arms nearly touched her chest.

And even though he made her crazy, damn him, every cell of

her body wanted him to lean closer, to bridge the inches separating them.

Do it, she told him silently, wishing he could read her mind. *Please, please, do it.*

He watched her carefully, his eyes trained on hers for so long that she almost began to wonder if he *would* make that move… *finally.*

And then his eyes shuttered.

"How many drinks have you had tonight?" he demanded. "Because you don't look sober. And if Nicole was your ride home, you are shit out of luck. She's obliterated."

Hillary closed her eyes for a moment, bracing against the rush of disappointment.

She had been a connoisseur of love since she'd first known the concept existed. As a writer, romance and happy-ever-afters were her stock in trade, so she'd read and researched and studied the condition the way an astronomer might study a distant planet, hoping that one day she'd get to experience it first-hand. She'd spent hours and hours dwelling on what being in love would feel like—the pulse-pounding heat of it, the soul-deep understanding, the feeling of connection, the longing to crawl deep beneath someone else's skin.

But for all her imaginings, she'd never dreamed that love could make a person feel so damn lonely or so out-of-control.

She opened her eyes and forced herself to smile.

"Three beers," she told Matteo calmly. "Oh, no, wait…"

She held up a finger and quickly downed the last of her beer.

"Make that four," she amended.

She saw him bite his lip, a sure sign that he was struggling to maintain control, and felt a perverse satisfaction.

"So help me, Tinker Bell," he warned, his green eyes blazing. "If you don't control yourself…"

And with that one word, she lost her mind.

"Don't. You. Call. Me. *That*!" she said, shoving her palm into his chest. "I am *nobody's* fairy princess, and definitely not *yours*. And if I don't control myself... *What?* Hmmm? Finish the sentence, Matteo, I dare you. What will you do?"

His eyes were focused on hers, and his jaw moved from side to side, but he didn't answer.

"Will you take me in hand? Punish me? Be my dominant?" she goaded. "No, of course you won't. Because I suggested that once before, to my everlasting shame. And you turned me down flat."

"And you know *why*," he said, his voice infuriatingly calm even as he leaned forward against her hand, close enough that she could feel his hot breath on her face. "I *don't* do long-term, I *don't* take advantage of girls who have some weird, misplaced hero-worship thing going on because I helped them out of a jam—"

"Hero-worship!" she sputtered. "Oh my God. You have totally lost your—"

"And," he continued, as though she hadn't interrupted, "I *don't* do girls who are eight fucking years *younger* than I am."

She shook her head at the utter stupidity of this statement.

"I can't give you what you *want* or what you *need*," he finished.

Can't? Or don't want to? But she didn't speak the thought aloud. She was pretty sure she already knew the answer, and had just enough pride to not want him to confirm it.

She was exhausted suddenly and could feel tears pricking the back of her eyelids.

"I'm not sure you have the first clue what I want or need," she told him wearily. "But it doesn't matter. You're *not* my dominant, Matt. So you *don't* need to know how many beers I've had. You *don't* get to make demands about how I'm going to get myself home. I'm a big girl and I'll take care of myself."

"Hillary," he began, his tone gentle.

His unexpected kindness was the last straw. She felt the traitorous tears starting to fall.

"Don't!" she warned him, hugging her arms around herself. "Don't be all nice to me. Not now. I can't handle it."

He uncrossed his arms and pulled her forward so that her forehead rested against the warmth of his chest.

"Ah, baby," he said, stroking his large, calloused hand over her short hair. "You've been so strong with everything that's happened these past few months."

She began to cry in earnest.

"But I don't *want* to be! You have n-no idea how h-hard it is to find a good Dom, Matt. I c-can't just walk into a club. I definitely can't go online again. I'm so sc-scared of meeting another guy like... *Marauder*," she finished in a whisper.

She felt his shoulders tense. She knew he didn't like remembering that night any more than she did.

"I don't *want* to feel this way—out of control and half-crazy. I don't *want* to be your problem anymore. But... I don't even know where to begin," she admitted.

Matteo was silent for a moment, then blew out a breath. "When you moved here, I promised you I'd be your friend, your big brother." He paused. "I'm thinking I've done a pretty shitty job of it."

Guilt reared its head and Hillary made a sound of denial. "I haven't exactly made it easy. I—"

He grabbed her shoulders and shook her gently until she lifted her head and met his eyes.

"When I fuck up, I say so," he told her. "But that ends now."

She frowned. "What does that mean?"

"It means that I'll find you a dom," he said, sliding his hand up to wrap around the back of her neck. "Someone that *I* know *I* can trust and, more importantly, that *you* can trust. Someone who can take care of you... give you everything you need."

She felt her eyes go wide.

"You? Are gonna play matchmaker? For me?" she repeated.

It sounded amazing. It also sounded like the worst kind of torture.

He pursed his perfect lips thoughtfully.

"Let's call it... Sourcing and vetting of qualified prospective dominants," he told her, his green eyes twinkling. "Matchmaking makes me think of my old Nana Angelico, trying to find nice Italian girls for her grandsons."

He surprised a watery laugh out of her.

"Oh, yeah. Definitely," she agreed with a sniffle, wiping her eyes with the back of her hand. "Sourcing and vetting is way more manly."

He chuckled. "Anyway, I've been around a while and know a lot of guys who are into the scene—some guys I've worked with at The Club, plus a few guys I know from the shop." His brow puckered. "I'll give it some thought and get you some possibilities by the end of the week."

Wait... A guy from The Club, one of the longest-running BDSM scenes in Boston, where Matt happened to be a part-time Dungeon Master and security guard, *or* a guy from *Inked*, the tattoo parlor where Matteo rented a table? This idea could have potential.

"Really?" she said. "You know, a guy from *Inked* might be nice."

He quirked an eyebrow. "Yeah? Why?"

"I've kinda got a thing for hot, tattooed guys, obviously," she told him. "*Mmm...* Definitely sexy."

His brow lowered, and the hand wrapped around her neck tightened momentarily before he dropped it to his side. "I'm pretty sure that's not the kind of thing a girl tells her brother."

But you're not my brother. Duh.

She laughed.

"But it's *exactly* the kind of thing a girl needs to tell the guy who's gonna *source and vet* her prospective doms," she informed him. "You know, maybe I need to get you a list of important criteria. Non-smoker. Can't live with his mother. Tall. Likes reading. Brown hair." She ticked off the items on her fingers.

"Yeah? You like brown hair?" he asked, smoothing a hand over his own short brown locks.

"Mmm… But maybe on the longer side. Like that football player, Julian Edelman. You know?"

He shook his head and pulled her out of the doorway, before removing the bucket and firmly closing the alley door.

"Anything else?" he asked, amused.

She pretended to think about it. "Nothing I can think of right now."

Matteo grabbed her elbow and gently led her back toward the party. "Then let's say our goodbyes to Dom and Heidi and get you home before you cause any more trouble, Tink."

She stopped short and her eyes narrowed.

"You know, there *is* one more thing," she informed him.

"Yeah?"

"The most important of *all* the criteria."

He sighed impatiently. "Okay, fine. Lemme hear it."

"Seriously, anyone who can't meet this condition is a non-starter."

"For God's sake, *what*?"

"He cannot, under any circumstances…" She paused dramatically. "Call. Me. *Tinker Bell*."

Then she sashayed back to the party, leaving him laughing behind her.

Chapter 2

Matteo opened a cabinet in the kitchen and pulled out two huge, drum-like black canisters he plunked on the counter a bit harder than was necessary.

"Chocolate malt or vanilla ice cream?" he asked over his shoulder.

His brother Dom was perched on a high stool at the counter in the kitchen.

"Like it matters? All those protein powders taste like shit. You can call it 'apple pie a la mode' or 'hot fudge sundae' and it's still soy and vitamins pulverized to within an inch of their lives."

Matteo turned a sardonic eye to his twin brother, and crossed his arms on his chest.

"I want to hear you bitch about protein powder? Chocolate or vanilla, asshole?"

Dom glared at him. "I don't bitch, dumbass. I state *facts*, and the fact remains, that stuff's shit no matter what you call it."

Matteo ripped open the chocolate, grabbed the scoop inside and dumped it into a shaker bottle.

"Fine. Make your own damn shake."

"Dude, lighten the hell up. I'll take chocolate." Dom sounded amused. "You know I'm not into the vanilla scene anyway."

Matteo snorted, scooping chocolate into a second bottle, topping them both with almond milk, and handing Dom his.

"Shake 'er up," he said. "You can *bitch* all you want about it, but if you want those ripped abs on your honeymoon, you'll down this after a workout."

Dom gave a mock salute, shook his bottle, then put it to his lips. He grimaced and shuddered, but downed the whole thing at once.

"Heidi will thank you," Dom muttered, pushing his empty bottle to Matteo. Matteo nodded, as he rinsed the bottles and put them in the dishwasher, a momentary pang of jealousy hitting him square in the chest. The fleeting thought crossed his mind that there was no one, save the anonymous girls he occasionally dommed when on duty at The Club, who would thank him for *his* efforts. Whatever. He felt comfortable in his own skin, knowing his body was at its peak. He loved the feeling of being strong and powerful, whether he had a submissive under his toned body or not.

It had been two weeks since Dom and Heidi's engagement party at *Cara* and at least three... maybe four... since he'd taken a girl to bed.

It was a fucking record.

"I gotta hit the shower and swing by the studio before we hit the tux place," he said on his way down the hall toward the bathroom.

"All right," Dom called down to him. "That's perfect. Heidi and Hillary are gonna meet us for burgers after. Heidi wants to see what we chose, and had to go get her shoes anyway."

Matteo froze, his hand on the knob of the linen closet door, his quest for nabbing a towel on the way to the shower momentarily forgotten.

Fucking *hell*.

Seriously, did people make up shit about twin intuition? Dom didn't have a fucking *clue*.

He squeezed his eyes shut, fuming silently, and yelled down the hallway to Dom, willing his voice to stay calm. "Heidi and Hillary? Why Hill?"

"She's the maid of honor. You know how that goes. Wedding shit's going down, she's there."

Matteo groaned as he opened the closet and towels spilled down on him. Damn, he really needed to tidy this place up. Maybe he needed to pay someone. He kept it clean—bathrooms wiped down with those Lysol things, floors mopped with the little jet mop contraption—but between his job at the tattoo parlor and stint at The Club, and the time he spent at the gym, he had little time for much else. He grabbed the towels and shoved them in haphazardly, taking one thick, hunter green one with him.

He didn't respond to Dom.

The last conversation he had with Dom involving *Hillary* and *Heidi* had been one absolute clusterfuck.

It was the night after Dom had proposed, just Hillary and Matteo, John, Paul, Heidi and Dom out to celebrate with a quiet meal. The girls and John had gone to the kitchen with Tess to look at some wedding cake thing or another, Paul had stepped outside to take a phone call and Dom and Matteo were left sitting at the table alone.

"You know she's crazy about you," Dom had said low, not one to pull punches. Matteo felt his eyes widen.

"Heidi? Well, yeah, I love her, too. It's gonna be great having her as a sister. You guys are..."

Dom shook his head, frowning. "Not Heidi, Matteo. Get your head outta your ass. *Hillary*."

Matteo drained his champagne glass and plunked it on the table.

"Come again?"

"She looks at you like a lovesick teenager," Dom said, and the playfulness in his eyes fled. "I'm gonna level with you, Matt. I know your reputation. I know how you play these things. You're a good man. You know I'd trust you with my life. You *know* that." He leaned in closer. "But this is *not* the place to fuck around. She's probably still mooning over you from saving her from that stint at Black Box. But I'm telling you now. Hillary's gonna be my sister-in-law." He paused. "Her sister will be my *wife.*"

Matteo nodded. Well, yeah. He knew that. Then why did his stomach sink to his toes, and a surge of adrenaline shoot through his arms like he wanted to shove his fist through the wall behind Dom's head?

"And I know Heidi asked you to watch out for her because she moved here and she's her younger sister and all that. I get it." Dom leaned closer to Matteo, his eyes dark, his voice low with a warning edge. "But you get me? Hillary is like my *sister.* You stay the hell away from her, or I swear to God, I'll kill you."

It would be a good fight, a brawl really, and he doubted Dom would *really* best him--Matteo was bigger and stronger—but he didn't want to find out.

But deep down inside, under the anger at Dom and pleasure with the confirmation that Hillary did indeed love him, and fury that her love for him would go unrequited... he knew Dom had a point.

And honestly, what could Matteo say to that?

Dom was right. Matteo *was* a player, with no interest whatsoever in things like rings, and weddings, and—*God!*—*commitment.*

And Hillary was Heidi's sister.

Sure, she was gorgeous, and funny, and sweet, and he knew she wanted to be a submissive. It would be great to actually *teach* her how to... but... no. Nope. He wasn't gonna go there.

He nodded to Dom.

"I get you," he said.

Dom's eyes narrowed. "You promise?"

"Promise."

And now, the gorgeous girl he'd carried out from that shit storm at Black Box, the one who'd put her head on his shoulder and cried while he took her to safety, his heart swelling with the desire to protect her and make her feel safe, the one he'd put on his very own couch, holding a glass of water to her shaking lips, tucking in a blanket over her little frame when she'd finally fallen asleep... she hated him now. And why?

Because he'd kept his word.

Why wouldn't she?

He wasn't gonna screw things up for Heidi and Dom. He'd *die* before he threw a wrench into the best thing that ever happened to his twin brother.

Hillary's feelings for him were no secret. She'd professed her love for him, and he turned her away. He had to. Out of duty. It killed him that her love for him would not be returned. She'd been so strong and brave, revealing her feelings for him. But he was bound to stay true to his word.

The tattoo around his bicep meant something to him. He'd been dead sober when he'd gotten it, and stared at in the mirror every single time he stepped out of the shower. It was the tag line he embraced as a young Marine, and it was engraved not just upon his arm, but his heart.

Death before Dishonor.

No. Hillary would be like... his *sister*.

Yeah, that was it. His sister.

His fucking *sister*.

He slammed into the shower, turning on the water so hot it scalded his skin, trying to wash all that was wrong and twisted and angry from his mind and body.

Even though he was tired, had pulled a twelve-hour shift earlier the day before, and had another night at The Club tonight, Matteo wished he was working at the studio. But no, instead he was going to the fucking *mall* to get *tuxedos* and eat burgers with Heidi, who he loved like a sister but who *would* go on and on about things like those candy almond things and wedding favors, and should the wedding cake be frosted *traditionally* or with fondant? But he'd also be eating with Hillary, who he'd successfully avoided ever since the night at *Cara* he'd stepped in it, promising her he'd find her a dom.

He'd promised to hook her up with a dom!

His brother would kick his ass. Or, at least he'd cause severe pain while *trying*.

What had he been fucking *thinking?*

Matteo sighed as they pulled into the parking lot of *Inked*.

When he'd come home from his last deployment, he'd been invited to temp at a tattoo parlor with his friend, Slay. Slay and Matteo had shared certain... *tastes*, they liked to say. The same taste in women. Same tastes in how they spent their free time when they were deployed. And Slay knew from the ample time they'd shared with one another that Matteo was an artist, gifted in graphic design. One night, when the two of them were grabbing a few cold ones at a small pub in Germany, Matteo had been doodling on a napkin.

"This shit's amazing," Slay said. "Matt, when you come back home with me, I'm bringing you to my brother. He's got a place near Boston. Tattoo joint. He's leasing private chairs and we can get in."

Six months later, on American soil, Matteo had needed little persuasion. Slay's brother helped him earn his spurs. Three years after arriving home, Matteo had an impressive portfolio, an apprenticeship under his belt, then a license, and one year after that, he'd spread his wings and rented out a private section of the studio with Slay. Slay worked a few nights a week as a bouncer at Black Box in the evening, his shift starting at ten, and though Matteo rarely saw him much in the club scene, they still ran into each other often during the day and managed to keep in touch.

Slay was the one who'd help him extract Hillary. Six foot four inches of pure, solid muscle, he was a force to be reckoned with, and though Black Box was known for deviant acts and drawing a seriously kinky crowd, Slay only worked there professionally, keeping his own personal life impeccable. Matteo knew he took his job as a sort of act of duty; his job as bouncer kept Black Box cleaner.

"You comin' in?" he asked Dom. Dom shook his head, his fingers flashing on his phone.

"Nah," he said. "Gotta send a few work emails. You gonna be long? We have an appointment at the tux place at six."

Matteo shook his head. "Five minutes," he said.

He left Dom in the car and entered *Inked*. Slay was intent on finishing a shoulder tat on a middle-aged guy with a beer gut and a sleeveless shirt. The guy's face was impassive, as he stared straight ahead, the only sound in the studio the steady *buzz* of Slay's tool. Slay's eyes met Matteo's as the door jangled, and Slay gave the slightest chin lift in greeting, not moving his hand as he put the finishing touches on his work.

"Be right with ya, Matt," Slay said, his deep, raspy voice carrying across the quiet room. Slay was taller than Matteo, heavier, having gained some weight after returning home from his deployment. He was bald, clean-shaven, had a chiseled jaw that was often clenched, and heavy, dark brows over dark eyes, and silver rings in his ears. He'd grown up on the streets of New York City, and was the toughest guy in a street brawl Matteo had ever met. He was also a dominant, though he never mixed business with pleasure and always met his submissives outside of Black Box.

Slay sat up. "You're all done," he said, wiping an alcohol swab over the man's arm and holding up a mirror for him to see. "You like it?"

The man nodded and grunted. "The Old Lady picked it out," he said. "She'll like it."

Slay nodded, not smiling, but Matteo knew him well enough he could tell he was pleased. Slay took pride in his work.

The man stood and shoved cash in Slay's hand before he shook it, and headed out of the shop, giving Matteo a chin lift on his way out.

"I've got your stuff," Slay said to Matteo, standing and stretching. Matteo followed him to the small break room in the back, a room so tiny it was almost a closet, complete with a small round table, a coffeemaker and little else. He picked up a small, black plastic bag and handed it to Matteo.

"Thanks, man," Matteo said. As an employee of Black Box, Slay had the opportunity to order equipment wholesale, so Matteo had placed an order. He wanted his own tools and equipment when he went to The Club tonight. Opening the bag, Matteo pulled out a small, silky mask—that would do perfectly—and a stout, burgundy leather strap. There were other tools he'd have at his disposal—paddles, cuffs, whips and canes—but he liked the strap. It was easy to hold, folded under his arm, or looped on his belt, and a quick snap of it could be used to garner attention when necessary.

It was also fucking sexy.

"You working tonight?" he asked Slay. Slay shook his head.

"Nah, I've got the weekend shift," he said. "Got tonight off, so I might see you at The Club." Unlike Black Box, The Club—simply named just that, The Club—was where doms like Slay liked to meet women. The Club was gentler, though still heavily invested in BDSM, with stricter rules, and tended to draw a younger, less experienced crowd than Black Box.

Matteo would be on as substitute Dungeon Master. Thursday

evening's Dungeon Master injured himself, and Matteo was the one who filled in when a Dungeon Master called in sick.

"Yeah, I'm subbing for the DM tonight," Matteo said. "Broke his arm in a biking accident."

Slay shook his head with a slight twitch of the lips. "Shame," he growled. "But a dom needs his fucking arm."

Matteo snickered. "Damn right."

On his way out, he thought about where he was going, and whom he'd see. He groaned. He couldn't avoid Hillary anymore, and what if she asked him about finding her a dom?

He'd promised her. And he always kept his word. He looked through the glass door to where Dom sat waiting in the car. He sighed. Damn it. It wouldn't be *exactly* going behind Dom's back. It wasn't even really *wrong*. Not like he was getting in bed with her.

He'd put it off long enough, and couldn't put it off much longer.

And who would be better to dom Hillary than Slay, the man Matteo worked with, military brother? Matteo had been with Slay long enough to know he knew his shit and he wouldn't hurt her.

"Hey, man," he said to Slay. "I gotta talk to you before I run. You got a minute?"

Cruel and unusual punishment.

Somewhere up there, someone had it in for him. It was really the only plausible explanation.

First, the discussion about introducing Slay to Hillary. He'd wanted to bite his own fucking tongue off, but he'd *told* her he would help her out, and he had to do *something* to get her to stop wanting to be with *him*. Maybe if Slay gave her what she needed, he and Hillary could go back to being... friends.

Had they ever just been friends?

Then, the tux gig. God, he hated trying on formal attire, and Heidi had given Dom some suggestions. Dom didn't know his ass from his elbow when it came to picking out tuxes, and the best Matteo could offer was a jeering recommendation that they go with the old-fashioned ones with top hats and tails, because the accessories with that ensemble included a cane. The accessories appealed to Matteo, for obvious reasons.

Dom nixed that idea.

"Heidi would blush the entire time, and we'd never get anything done," he said, shaking his head with a wicked gleam in his eye.

Matteo could only imagine what it was about a cane that would make her blush, but whatever. He was useless in the tux department. So they were dressed up, and the sales person, an older, matronly lady with graying hair and bushy eyebrows, fussed and primped, murmuring how handsome they looked in *gray* and how nice their trim waists looked with *these* cummerbunds or vests.

Torture. Pure torture. And it only got worse.

After *that* particular form of torture, Heidi had texted Dom and Dom had dragged him to the other end of the mall where, unbeknownst to him, Hillary was trying on dresses. There was a small, privately owned dress shop that specialized in one-of-a-kind formal gowns. Dom told Matteo that Heidi and Hillary's mom had given Heidi a blank check and told her she would buy both Heidi's gown and Hillary's. The girls wanted Dom and Matteo's opinions.

So there he stood when Hillary walked out of the dressing room.

When her eyes met his, he expected her to look angry, as she'd grown withdrawn the past few months, and who could blame her if she was pissed off at him now? *He'd* be pissed off with himself. He'd made her a promise, then completely ignored her. But she didn't look angry. She looked... apologetic?

And fucking *gorgeous*.

She stepped out to where there were benches in the waiting area outside the dressing room in the little shop. The dress looked somehow soft and shimmery, and though he didn't know the material, he did know it begged to be touched. The color of spun gold, strapless, banded around her small but curvy torso, with an accent band around her slim waist, the hem hitting just above her knees.

Heidi had taken Dom to the other side of the store to see a tiara that she loved, and Matteo and Hillary stood silently, gazing at one another. She took a step toward him, shyly tucking her hands behind her back, one foot behind the other as if she were prepared to curtsy.

"Do you like it?" she murmured, her eyes focused steadily on him, pleading.

Like it?

He could not stop himself. How could he? He wanted to gather her in his arms and kiss the flush of her cheeks, feel the softness of her dress as he stripped it away...

Smiling softly, he reached out to tuck a strand of hair behind her ear. She bit her lip and her breath caught as he lifted her hand to his lips and kissed her fingers.

"Gorgeous," he murmured, intentionally making sure she didn't know if he referred to the dress or to her.

The dress was *nice*, of course.

But *she* was gorgeous.

They heard Heidi and Dom approaching, and both immediately pulled away and stood straighter, Hillary pretending to look at the shoes lined up on shelves on the wall behind her.

"Hey, Hill, that's a pretty dress!" Dom said, and Matteo wanted to *deck* him.

Pretty?

Dress?

"I totally think you should get it!" Heidi said, clapping her hands together, and as they discussed shoes and accessories and all that shit, the moment was gone, whisked away by frivolities and duty.

Thank *God.*

She bought the dress, and Dom drove them all to Roadhouse, their favorite burger joint, Heidi sitting shotgun, Hillary and Matteo sitting in the backseat, so far apart from one another they were each flush against the doors on either side.

Matteo picked up his phone and texted her.

Her phone beeped and when she read it was from him, she stifled a giggle.

What's up? She texted.

Remember I made you a promise at Cara?

Yeah. I remember. I thought you were the one who hadn't.

Well, that stung, but he deserved it.

Nah, babe. I've been working on it. Working on it. Yeah, he'd been working on it, going through every single dom he knew, every single dom *possibility,* and systematically discarding each one in turn as wrong for Hillary.

And the next words he typed just about killed him, but he had to. For her. He inhaled.

So, I found you a dom.

He expected her eyes to light up, or at least a smile to flit across her face, but she remained impassive. What the hell?

Yeah?

Yeah. Guy named Slay. You met him the night I got you out of Black Box. Served in the Marines with me. Experienced. Tough, big guy, but a good one.

She put her phone down and her eyes met his across the car. They didn't speak for a minute and he raised his eyebrows. He'd rather cut off his left nut than let her be dommed by some other guy, and this was killing him. Didn't she know this was killing him? Then why was her chin thrust in the air and her eyes flashing at him? Jesus. She looked back at her phone and her fingers flew.

He jumped as his phone buzzed. That was quick. He read her message.

Thanks. Think he can handle me?

Handle her? He pursed his lips. He'd done his job, gotten her a dom, and now he was done.

Yeah. He's got experience handling fairies, Tink.

He stifled a groan as her leg shot out and she kicked his shin. He glared at her and typed so fast, he had to erase and rewrite his message four times.

You are SO LUCKY you are not mine or you wouldn't sit FOR A WEEK!

She looked *smug*, the little brat. His phone buzzed one more time.

Well, then. Since you can't SPANK my ass you can KISS my ass.

He looked at her through eyes so narrow they were little more than slits as he shut his phone off and shoved it in his pocket.

He'd give her Slay's number, and be done with it, but she'd have to behave herself first.

Chapter 3

Hillary hitched her purse strap higher on her shoulder. She quickly looked down at the text message on her phone and then back up at the nondescript brownstone with its sedate-looking first floor bar. *826 Queensborough.* This was the place. "The Club." Supposedly. She wasn't sure exactly what she had expected a BDSM club to look like, but her imagination probably would've run more to neon signs and black leather, rather than a quiet, upscale neighborhood of homes and restaurants.

She frowned, wishing for the first time that she had agreed to let Slay pick her up at her place. It had been clear from his texts that he hadn't been keen on the idea of meeting her here, of letting her arrive here alone, but it had been weirdly important to her to get here under her own power. Proof that she was a big girl, capable of handling her dates on her own, even if she *had* agreed to let Matt set her up. Proof that she was a competent, independent woman, albeit one who happened to be here to meet a dominant and maybe become his submissive.

Plus, letting him come to her apartment presented other logistical challenges, like fact that her super-protective big sister and almost-brother-in-law lived practically next door, in Dom's apartment, while she lived just across the alley, in Heidi's old place.

Reason 477,522 that I need to finish writing my damn novel and move out of Heidi's apartment, she reminded herself.

So, what now? Text Slay? Head into the bar? Either was preferable to standing on the sidewalk propping up the streetlight for the rest of the night.

As Hillary bit her lip in indecision, the door to the bar opened, spilling out a low stream of rock music and a pair of patrons. The woman of the pair was already leaning against the man drunkenly, despite the fact that it wasn't quite 7:00 PM and the sun hadn't fully set. Hillary gave the woman a polite smile, and the woman winked and grinned lasciviously, earning her a frown from her companion. As they passed Hillary, the man reached down and smacked the woman's bottom firmly.

"Behave," he commanded her in a low voice.

Oh.

Well, then.

This *was* the place.

Without giving herself a chance to think about it further, she walked down the three stone steps to the entrance, and pulled open the door.

It was much smaller than she had imagined. A bar bordered by leather stools ran along the entire front wall of the narrow space, and there were a few round tables and chairs against the back wall, but all were unoccupied. Two men talking in low voices flanked a doorway at the back corner of the room, while a pretty bartender wiped the gleaming bar top.

No Slay anywhere.

This was The Club? The place where Matteo spent all his free time? For God's sake, why?

Hillary hitched her purse strap up again, fighting the urge to just walk out and go home. This was all Matteo's fault. She hadn't spoken to him since the day they'd met at the mall and he'd finally, grudgingly, given her Slay's number. If he hadn't forced her hand the other day by bringing up this stupid matchmaking business when she'd *thought* they were having a *moment*, if he hadn't been all charming and heartbreakingly kind to her the night of the engagement party, if he had just *wanted* her the way she wanted him....

But he didn't.

And she had to stop thinking about this shit.

So... Okay, fine. She was going to respect his wishes. She was going to give this date a serious shot. She'd wait for Slay.

"Uh, hi," she said to the bartender. "Could I please have a beer? Sam Adams?"

The bartender, who seemed barely old enough to drink, flicked her long, blonde ponytail and looked at Hillary curiously. "Uh... Sure, I guess. Yeah. ID?"

Hillary dug through her purse and produced her license, while the bartender grabbed a beer from the cooler behind her.

"So," she said, nodding at Hillary's license as she set the bottle on a small white napkin. "You're waiting for someone?"

Wow. Was it that obvious?

"Yeah. A... guy," Hillary said. She forced herself to stop fidgeting with her stupid purse strap.

The bartender smiled and nodded again, like this was to be expected. "He know you're here?"

"Who, the guy? No. Not yet. I mean, Slay knows he's meeting me, but I didn't text him when I got here. Maybe I should?"

"S-Slay? You're meeting Slay?" The blonde's smile fell.

"Yeah?" Hillary agreed, confused. "You know him?"

"Oh. No. Nope. I mean..." She looked flustered and Hillary felt a pang of sympathy. "Yeah, but not really. Just... you know, from when he comes in. I, uh, I've just never seen him bring in a guest before. Until you."

She appraised Hillary over the top of the bar, taking in everything from the pastel-colored tips of Hillary's hair to the short, clingy purple dress that cinched at Hillary's waist. The woman frowned, glancing down at her own plain t-shirt and skirt. Then she seemed to remember herself.

"Oh, I'm Alice," she told Hillary, offering her hand.

"Hillary," Hillary said, clasping her hand firmly.

Alice nodded and smiled in a half-hearted way. "Well, Slay's already here. I-I mean, I *think* I might have seen him come in," she said. And Hillary could swear she saw the other woman blush.

"Hey, Donnie!" Alice called. The taller of the two men in the back looked up. "Tell Slay his guest is here?" The man nodded and disappeared through the door.

"They can't let you into The Club on your own if you're not a member, but he'll find Slay for you," she explained to Hillary.

"This... *this* isn't The Club?" Hillary asked, looking around in confusion.

Alice let out a peal of laughter that lit up her blue eyes and made her look even sweeter.

"Not even close. The entrance to The Club is back there." She waved a hand toward the doorway where Donnie's companion still stood.

"This is, like..." Alice paused for a moment, thinking. "You know how in those spy movies, there's always a front that the spies use? Oh, don't mind us, we're just a bunch of harmless accountants or movie producers or whatever?"

Hillary raised one eyebrow. "The bar is your secret cover?"

"Well, not exactly *secret*," Alice amended. "But you might say that this is The Club's innocent vanilla exterior. By club policy, we're not allowed to let just anyone in to the main club, only members and their guests. This front room is a place for people to meet up before they enter the chaos back there."

Hillary swallowed.

The chaos back there.

Images filled her mind. The flash of strobe lights punctuating the darkness as she followed Marauder through the throngs of people on the dance floor at Black Box, half-naked bodies pressing in on all sides. The demonstrations, the public punishments, the eerie silence of the soundproofed room...

"Hillary?"

Hillary looked up at the sound of her name, then found she had to look up some more. Oh my word, this man was huge. She could feel her eyes widening as she tried to take him in.

She had only the haziest recollections of the man from the night he helped Matteo save her—a vague impression that he was a big guy, gruff and commanding. Her memory didn't do him justice.

He was bald, his head completely shaved, in a way that might have looked ridiculous, had his head not been perched on a neck as thick as a tree-trunk. The silver hoops in each ear and the variety of tattoos all over his hands and arms screamed *dangerous*. His black t-shirt stretched tightly across the most muscular chest and arms she'd ever seen—possibly even larger than Matteo's, and his booted feet were braced slightly apart, as though he were perpetually ready for a fight. Even his face was hard, his jaw clenched firmly, betraying no emotion.

She took a deep breath and prayed for courage.

"You must be Slay!" she said, extending her hand politely. "Hi! It's very nice to meet you."

Slay looked at her extended hand for a moment. His lips twitched. She noticed that his eyes were brown, like caramel, and fringed with long lashes. Insanely pretty eyes for a man this formidable. Somehow that realization calmed her nerves.

"Real nice to meet you, too, honey," he said, his voice deep and gruff, and his enormous hand engulfed hers. "Matt's told me a bit about you."

Hillary nodded. "He... um... he didn't tell me much about

you. I was kinda out of it, but I know you were there last spring, when…"

Slay's face grew stony again. "Yeah," he said.

Hillary swallowed. "I just wanted to say thank you. You know, sorta get that out of the way before we, um…" She glanced at the back corner of the bar, where Donnie and the other man had resumed their positions.

"You do *not* thank me for that," he told her. "I'm sorry it happened. I'm glad I was able to help. And I wish I'd been able to tear that motherfucker's dick off so he wouldn't even think about doing that to anyone else."

Well. Alrighty then.

Hillary nodded and Slay's eyes softened.

"So, you want a tour of the club?"

She straightened her shoulders and smiled.

"Yeah. Yes. Definitely."

He grabbed her beer and placed it in her hand, then put his arm around her waist and steered her toward the door. But they hadn't gone more than a few steps before he stopped and called back over his shoulder.

"Alice. You staying out of trouble?"

Hillary looked back in time to see Alice's pretty face scowl as she glared at Slay's broad back.

"Not much opportunity for anything else when I'm stuck out here," Alice muttered, just loud enough for them to hear.

Hillary could swear she saw Slay smothering a smile. Then he nodded to Donnie, and the other guard pulled open the rear door. They stepped into The Club.

The music was much louder back here, the bass thumping. It was another bar area, twice as large as the one out front, with several hallways leading off it. And unlike the bar out front, this room was packed with people. But Hillary was relieved to see that unlike the writhing crush of bodies she remembered from Black Box, this room was well lit, and fairly tame. People were dressed casually, sexily, much the way Hillary herself was dressed. She smoothed a hand down her stomach and felt her tension relax a notch.

Slay led her to a table on the far side of the room and nudged her onto a chair in the corner before taking the chair next to her. He caught the bartender's eye and lifted his chin, and the woman immediately rushed over with a bottle of whiskey and a glass.

She poured a shot without making eye contact with Slay, and set it neatly on a white napkin.

"On my tab," Slay said, and the woman nodded, her eyes never rising above Slay's chin before she scurried away.

Oh. Wow.

Hillary felt her stomach flip. *That was hot.*

"So," Slay said. He dragged his chair closer and leaned over her just a little, so the breadth of his chest blocked out the rest of the bar. It made Hillary's heart race, and she could *almost* pretend that it was in a good way. She took a nervous sip of her beer.

"We'll start our tour here. Hang out and relax for a bit, since you look like you're about to faint or some shit." He winked.

Hillary bit her lip. "*Sorry*. I'm sorry. It's just all kinda… new and overwhelming."

"I don't mind, honey," he told her seriously. "It's sweet. But you shoulda let me pick you up at your house."

She opened her mouth to argue, then stopped herself. She'd told herself that she'd make a real effort tonight, and that probably didn't involve pissing off a potential dom by arguing about trivial things.

She closed her mouth and nodded instead.

He looked amused again.

"I'll let you pick where you want to go from here," he told her, speaking into her ear so that she could hear over the thrum of the music. "The Club is actually the entire building we're standing in, plus the building behind us—three floors above ground, one below."

Hillary felt her eyebrows lift.

"Top floor has private rooms. Don't think we need to see *those* tonight," he said, leaning back to watch her reaction.

Hillary blushed and shook her head. *Definitely* not. Probably never. She couldn't even imagine…

"Right, didn't think so," he agreed, capturing her attention again. "So, there are various demonstrations going on downstairs."

Once again, he paused to take in her reaction.

Shit. That wasn't really her thing, either. She couldn't imagine standing next to this man while watching… But she didn't want him to think she was a total prude.

She forced herself to smile and nod eagerly.

He chuckled at that, and a full-on grin that transformed his whole face for a moment into something friendly and open.

"Yeah, I didn't think you'd wanna do that either," he told her, able to see right through her false enthusiasm. Hillary giggled in relief.

"There's a dance floor back there, plays mostly dance and house music," he said, hooking a thumb toward one hallway.

His tone of disgust made Hillary giggle again.

"So, you're a big fan of dance music, then?" she asked.

He raised one eyebrow. "Like, totally," he deadpanned.

Hillary snickered and felt another knot in her belly release.

"There's another dance floor that plays mostly pop stuff, some rock," he continued, hooking his thumb toward another hallway. "That one's not *as* bad."

"I *do* like dancing," Hillary offered, smiling.

"We can head back there, if you want," he told her. "FYI, *I* don't dance. But I'm happy to watch *you* do your thing for a while."

Heat flared in his eyes and made Hillary blush again. She

looked down at the tabletop and traced the wood grain intently with her fingernail.

It felt nice, this attention, it did. He seemed genuinely interested in her, and she found that she really liked him. But somehow she was still uneasy. Being with him like this, feeling his warm breath on her neck, felt *wrong* for some reason she couldn't put her finger on.

"Or," Slay said, putting his large hand on top of hers to stop her fidgeting. "We could just stay here and talk for a while. Get to know each other."

Her eyes shot to his and she smiled gratefully. Slay's lip twitched.

"So cute," he muttered.

"So, um…You said that Matteo had told you about me," she started. "What did he already tell you?"

Slay shrugged.

"The basics. You're a waitress at Tony's place, you just graduated from college, you're pretty new to the scene. You're not interested in getting any more tattoos, so I shouldn't get any ideas." He looked pointedly at the star tattoos on each of her wrists, and Hillary smiled.

"And," Slay continued, "he said you need a dom."

The words, spoken so casually, slammed into Hillary. This was no ordinary blind date. This man was a dom. If things went well, he would be... *her* dom. She tried to imagine it, but failed.

"Oh, and he gave me your description. I didn't remember much about you from that night last spring."

Hillary nodded.

"He said, 'Look for Tinker Bell'," Slay said, chuckling. "Easy enough." He leaned back and winked at her.

She inhaled sharply.

Oh. My. God. She was going to *kill* Matteo.

As if her murderous thoughts had conjured him, Matteo walked into the room right then. Just the sight of him made

Hillary's stupid heart start pounding faster than it had all evening.

He stalked up to the bar and signaled to the bartender, much as Slay had. His jaw was set, his green eyes were stern and he spoke sharply to the woman behind the bar, who nodded without meeting his eyes. He spoke again and the woman handed him a bottle of water. He turned and stood with his back to the bar, his eyes roving over the scene...

Until they landed on her.

And then Slay.

And then the beer she clutched nervously in her hands.

And they narrowed.

He pushed himself off the bar and stalked towards them.

"Hey, man," he greeted Slay, exchanging chin lifts. "Tink behaving herself?"

His gaze fastened on hers, and his green eyes flashed. She'd almost swear he looked angry. For a second she wondered what had him so upset, and wanted to make him smile.

Before she remembered that she was pissed off, too.

Without waiting for Slay to answer, he grabbed the chair on the other side of her and turned it around, straddling it. He leaned across the table and spoke to Slay.

"You two getting to know each other?" he asked.

Hillary stiffened.

"Yes," she told him, before Slay had a chance to respond. "We are. And I was just about to share with Slay that I absolutely *hate* being called Tinker Bell."

She leaned closer to Slay. "It's a short-girl thing, you know? I'm kinda sensitive about it."

She gave Slay her most flirtatious smile.

Matteo scowled.

"So, you work with Matteo?" she asked Slay, taking a sip of her beer. "I feel sorry for you."

Slay chuckled. "Honey, you don't know the half of it."

"What's that supposed to mean?" Matteo demanded.

Slay turned to Hillary.

"We were in the service together, you know? Matt's a good man. The best. A talented artist. No one I'd rather have watching my six in here or out there. But, God, the *singing*."

Hillary choked. "The... *what?*"

Matteo glowered threateningly at Slay. "Dude, don't go there."

Slay only laughed. "You've never heard him sing? God, I thought he had a song for every occasion. The first week we were in—" he hesitated and exchanged a look with Matteo. "Well, never mind where we were. But it was hot, miserable, exhausting. We had sand in parts of our bodies where sand doesn't belong. Tempers were running high. It was impossible to relax. All of a sudden one night, right when I thought the shit was about to hit the fan, this guy starts *singing*... Disco hits from the 70s!"

Matteo growled and Slay cracked up.

Hillary shook her head, sure she'd heard wrong.

"D-disco hits?" she repeated, looking to Matteo for confirmation, but he shook his head.

"Gloria Fucking Gaynor," Slay confirmed, his big body shaking with laughter at the memory. "*I... I will survive,*" he belted out in a crazy falsetto that had people at nearby tables looking over at them with wide eyes. "And it worked. Before you know it, everyone in that mess hall was singing along, laughing at his crazy ass."

"I... wow," Hillary said.

She stared at Matteo, who had folded his arms across his chest and was watching her digest that information. Did he worry that this would change her opinion of him? Make him seem less intimidating, less dom-ish? Because it didn't. If anything, it made it even harder to keep her heart from bursting out of her chest. There was so much about him that she didn't know, more than she had imagined. She wanted to know *all* of it, hear every story.

"I thought you were supposed to be getting to know *Hillary*, not reliving ancient history," Matteo grumbled. "She tell you she's a writer?"

Hillary's image of Matteo singing promptly dissolved and she stared at him in horror. It wasn't that she wasn't proud of being a writer, or of the things she wrote. It just… wasn't something she chose to share with everyone. It was intensely personal, and people could be so damn *judgy*.

Matteo returned her stare and cocked his head, a subtle dare.

After a moment of uncomfortable silence, Slay spoke. "You're a writer?"

Hillary stopped plotting Matteo's murder and looked at Slay thoughtfully. Given the fact that they were already meeting in a BDSM club, she figured maybe she could be a little less reserved than she normally was.

"I am," she agreed. "I write… romance."

Slay's eyebrow shot high. "You're shittin' me."

She smiled. "Nope."

"So, like… knights and ladies and stuff? Or, um, the hard-core stuff?" he asked her. Then, seeing Matteo's raised eyebrow, he said defensively, "I don't live under a rock, asshole. My grandma used to read them. And now my sister's all over Face-book about Fifty Fucking Shades."

He and Matteo both grimaced.

Hillary giggled.

"Well, um… closer to the second kind, I guess. My high school lit teacher told me to write what I like to read, so…" She shrugged and smiled. "It's mostly erotic romance with some dominance and submission elements."

His eyes widened. "Shit. So, with the steamy sex scenes and… everything?"

Hillary stifled a laugh. This big, burly, tank of a dominant looked a little bit shocked.

"And everything," she agreed.

It wasn't *precisely* true. She was able to get the sex scenes down, all right, but lately the steam was sadly lacking and she had no clue how to fix it. It was like some weirdly specific form of writer's block. And it meant that her recent novel was still sitting on her computer, unfinished.

"And you're fine with this?" Slay asked. This was directed at Matteo, and Slay looked like he was simultaneously horrified and impressed.

Matteo scowled.

"Matteo doesn't get to have an opinion," Hillary interrupted. "He's not my dom." It was a knee-jerk reaction, and as she said the words, she felt the pain of them all over again. But then she realized the implication of what Slay was saying.

"Do you mean you wouldn't want your sub to write romance?"

Slay shrugged. "I don't know. Doesn't it draw a lot from personal experience? I wouldn't want people to read that shit and be speculating about my private business."

Hillary nodded slowly, wishing Matt hadn't brought it up.

Matteo snorted. "She writes under a pen name, idiot. Besides, there's not a damn thing wrong with *writing* about it. We *live* it for Christ's sake."

Slay shrugged again. "Didn't say there was anything *wrong* with it. Just not my thing."

Matteo narrowed his eyes. "I can't believe you're being judgmental about this, shithead."

Hillary held up a placating hand.

"Matt, stop. It's fine. I get it," she told Slay. "No big deal. Everyone has a different comfort zone."

Slay nodded. "So, um… You want another beer?" he asked, clearly trying to turn the conversation.

"Yeah, sure!" Hillary said, finishing the last sip from her bottle. "I'd love another."

"How many have you had?" Matteo asked her. Then he turned to Slay angrily. "Have you even *asked* her how many she's had? Do you even *know?*"

Slay sat back in his seat and folded his arms, eyeing Matteo speculatively, but he said nothing. So Hillary stepped into the breach.

"Matteo! This was my only beer. I am *fine*," she said firmly. "Why are you always so obsessed with how much I've had to drink, anyway?" She smiled, inviting the two stony-faced men to smile with her, trying to play peacemaker.

"It's not about how much you've had to drink," Matteo said. "I could give a shit if you get drunk, as long as you're *safe*. That means being in a safe environment and having a safe way home."

Hillary sighed. Why did he have to be so wonderfully protective and kind, even while he was essentially trying to give her to another guy? He made her head spin way more than the beer did.

"You think I wouldn't protect her?" Slay challenged. "Are you kidding me with this shit?"

Matteo shrugged, and the tension around the table ratcheted up a notch.

This was not good. Not remotely good.

"Excuse me, sir." A brunette, dressed in a white t-shirt and leather skirt like those worn by all the bartenders, stood at Matteo's elbow and addressed him breathlessly. "You asked me to let you know if that *certain person* was causing trouble. He is, sir. He's making a scene in the Red Room. Hank has him locked down, but can't get him out without some assistance."

Matteo looked torn for a moment, glancing back and forth from Hillary to Slay to the hallway beyond the bar. "Yeah, fine. Thanks, Deb. I'll take care of it."

The woman nodded and hesitated, staring hard at Hillary for

a second before finally hurrying away. Matteo reluctantly pushed himself to his feet.

"No. You know what? *I* will go give Hank a hand," Slay said, standing up abruptly. "I'm in the mood to crack some fucking heads."

He glared at Matteo.

Then he turned to Hillary and bent low, whispering in her ear.

"It was very nice to meet you, honey. You've got my number. Feel free to use it anytime."

He pressed a kiss to her forehead that felt more brotherly than any interaction she'd ever had with Matteo, and she realized what had felt off about his physical proximity to her all night: He wasn't Matteo, and Matteo was the only one she wanted in that way. Ignoring her feelings wasn't making them go away. She was more in love with him than ever.

Shit.

She was an idiot.

And she wasn't the only one.

"So…" Matteo said, nodding his head as Slay stalked away. "That went pretty well."

Hillary's jaw dropped. "Are you serious? That was a *disaster*."

"Well, in a way you're right. And that's mostly my fault. Sorry, babe," he said sincerely. He shook his head in disgust and took a deep drink from his water bottle.

She sighed. "It's okay." Given that she was in love with Matteo, she and Slay had pretty much been doomed from the start.

"No," he told her. "It's not. There are certain standards of behavior, you know? Certain things that are just never acceptable. You shouldn't forgive me so easily."

She sighed again. "Yeah, well, don't be too hard on yourself. You can't help being protective…"

"But that's just it!" he said. "You trusted me to find you a decent guy, and I promised I would. And I had no idea that Slay was such a judgmental asshole. I'm sorry I set you up with that guy, babe."

Hillary pressed her lips together. "That's what you're sorry for?" She wanted to laugh. She wanted to cry.

"Well, yeah," he said, as though this should be obvious. "But don't be too discouraged. I mean, finding you the right dom is going to be as much about figuring out what we *don't* want as what we *do* want. You know?"

"What *we* want?" she repeated, laughter winning over tears.

"Next time I will give a lot more thought to the dom I source and vet for you. I don't know what I was thinking, picking Slay." He shook his head again.

"You... you think there's a better dom out there?" she asked. "Better than your best friend, a guy you served with, and work with, and sang disco hits with?"

Matteo shrugged.

"Who *are* you going to trust if you can't trust the guy who had your back for a decade?" she pressed. "You trust him with your *life*, Matt," she reminded him.

"Yeah, but I don't trust him with *you*!" he exploded. He seemed to realize what he had said, and cast around wildly for escape.

Hillary's heart was beating so fast she could hear it over the loud thump of the music. It felt like the last few months of her life had been leading her to this very moment.

"Then I think I should probably find my *own* dom," she told him. "I release you from your promise."

"What? No!" he argued. "Absolutely not."

"Yes," she said firmly. "I'm going to go on Match. Or Fetlife. Somewhere. Maybe I'll get a membership here, explore the place myself."

"Jesus, Hillary," he whispered. It was almost a plea.

But she couldn't back down. Wouldn't.

"It's the only way, isn't it? There's not going to be a person on earth you trust to take care of me, to be my dom."

He looked at her, straight at her, an agonized, hungry look in his beautiful green eyes. She could feel his leg bouncing wildly beneath the tabletop, faster and faster.

Hillary's breath caught in her throat at the intensity of his focus. God, what she wouldn't give to be able to read his mind! Was he dreaming up some excuse, some argument, that might change her decision? Scrolling through his memory bank for another potential dom? Or was there even the *slightest* chance that he felt the same pull that she felt, the same feeling of rightness, of inevitability, when they were together, despite all his protests?

What would it mean if he felt that way?

And, God, what would she do if he didn't?

The silence dragged on and she clutched her hands together beneath the table, feeling dread pool in her belly.

But then his leg stopped bouncing.

He closed his eyes for a moment, then opened them.

And nodded.

"You're right," he said slowly. "I don't trust anyone else. I'm going to have to do it myself."

Chapter 4

What the actual *fuck* had he been thinking?

I'm going to have to do it myself.

First, Dom was going to kill him. He'd probably beat him to a bloody pulp first, and if Slay was around he'd probably be oh so happy to lend a hand, *then* he would kill him, and when he was good and thoroughly dead, Matteo would go straight to hell.

But the way her eyes lit up. Oh, God, her eyes. They'd squeezed shut quickly, and when they opened they were brighter, trusting, even a little damp.

Shit.

He knew how to be a dom. He had done this for years and was well versed in meeting the needs of a submissive. And hell, he knew that girl well. He knew that she was sweet but edgy, and the day after she'd been rescued from Black Box, when he'd taken her to the police station, she'd sat in the chair giving her report with a voice that didn't waver, articulately and pointedly relating every detail of what happened, even when the officer in charge asked probing questions that would've made other girls cringe or falter. Not Hillary. Getting her out of that horrific scene and being the one to take her home had satisfied a need deep within him. Rescuing her had been the first nail in the coffin. Her willingness to trust him and the way she relaxed around him was the second nail. The third nail was, absolutely, the way she intelligently explained to the officer how the scene was supposed to have been consensual, and somehow hearing her explain her engagement in BDSM activities seemed like the most natural thing in the world. Learning who she really was—sweet, but strong, capable and brilliant, fun to be with, sexy beyond his wildest imagination, and—yeah. Oh yeah, he was a total goner.

But he'd given his word to Dom, and *now* what was he going to do? He mulled it over, while she sat patiently, her finger trailing a pattern on the condensation of her beer bottle. Without conscious thought, he reached for her hand, the back of his left hand grazing the table so that his palm was face up, the slightest bend in his fingers welcoming her hand. Her eyes were focused on the table, as she gingerly placed her hand in his and he placed his right hand atop hers so that both his hands were holding her one.

"We can make this work," he said, more to convince himself than her. "But so help me God, if you breathe a word of this to Dom or Heidi, you won't sit for a week. And you know this is just to help you, right?"

She blinked. "What do you mean?" And she tried to pull her hand away, but he held fast.

Shit would be on *his* terms now.

"You need me to help you," he said. "Reach your goals, take care of yourself, learn how to be obedient and submissive. But *no sex.*"

A look flitted across her face but she quickly masked it with a sarcastic roll of her eyes as she pursed her lips at him. "Aw, *shucks,*" she said. "I was so hoping you'd nail me tonight."

His hands tightened on hers, and he realized with a bit more satisfaction than he really should have, that he now had the ability to do something about her wise cracks. He dropped his voice and leaned in closer, making sure her eyes were focused on him and he had her undivided attention.

"That's ten," he said.

She inhaled and swallowed.

"What's that supposed to mean?" she hissed, as if she were afraid of being overheard. "You won't!"

She was gonna sass him, too? He narrowed his eyes at her.

"You do *not* roll your eyes at me or talk back. Am I clear? We're in a BDSM club, Hillary. You do it again, I push my chair out and take you across my lap right here. Understood?"

Her eyes widened, but she nodded.

"Okay," she whispered, frowning. "Should I be calling you 'sir'?"

"Normal day to day? No. When I correct you? Absolutely."

She merely nodded again. The idea of her addressing him as sir... *God.*

Where to begin? The first thing he wanted to do was get her the hell out of The Club. It was a place where people met and played, and though he'd had plenty of nights where play was at the top of his list, the idea of the other men looking at her... hell no. His adrenaline surged as he got to his feet, still holding her hand.

"You're going to spank me now?" she squeaked, and he realized that she mistook his sudden moves as an indication that he was prepared to punish her. He softened, tugging her hand, pulling her a bit closer and one of his arms snaked around her shoulder.

"Not now, honey," he said gently. "My shift is over, but there's a protocol I need to follow before I leave. So I need to go and make sure that's taken care of before I take you back to my place, but when I do, you *are* getting a spanking."

He watched as she swallowed and nodded. She liked hearing him say he would spank her. Hell, he liked the idea of spanking her. But this was not a game. The girl needed a real spanking, and he would give her what she needed.

It wasn't just because she rolled her eyes at him, though he couldn't let that go uncorrected. The most basic element of any D/s dynamic Matteo would partake in was the expectation of his submissive's respect and obedience. Other doms might warn first, but in this case, he felt it would be best to set her straight. And she was *long* overdue for a good spanking. It wouldn't be just punitive, though. He needed to clear the air and establish their roles.

She trotted to keep up with his long strides, and he knew what was coming next, as it was common enough it was almost predictable. The first mention of a punishment, and they would ask questions, push, and test, some harder than others. It was an almost necessary step when establishing roles. Did he *really* mean what he said?

"Are you sure you're going to spank me tonight?" she asked, as they walked past the bar to the office, a small room tucked behind the bar. "I mean, we haven't even set ground rules yet, and you're just jumping in, and—"

To a dom new to the scene, the questioning was sometimes frustrating, but Matteo knew where it was coming from. He'd spent long hours learning from submissives, both those he dommed and those he didn't, learning from experienced doms and dommes, and witnessing firsthand the results of being consistent, firm, and dependable. Even though most submissives didn't really *like* being punished, they needed to know their dominant meant what he said. So when doubts began to emerge, they would often push, some harder than others, but honest questioning was part of the normal routine. They needed consistency, dependability, and most of all, to know they were willingly relinquishing control to someone *strong* and worthy.

He pulled her to a quiet spot and pushed her in front of him so that her back was flush against the wall. Leaning in, he pinned her with no more than the heat of his body, one of his arms above her head, resting on his forearm, the other still holding her hand.

"Known each other a while now, haven't we?" he asked low.

She swallowed and nodded, clearly intimidated by his physical posture and their near proximity. Good. This was time, now, for her to learn to focus on him and obey, and a little intimidation went a long way.

"Yes," she said, and as he stepped a little closer, she quickly amended it with, "Yes, sir!"

"Do I like it when you roll your eyes at me or talk back?"

She shook her head silently.

"In fact, what have I said to you more than once?"

She swallowed. "Um...about what? I mean there are lots of things you've said to me, and I—"

He leaned closer. "About being a *brat*, Hillary."

Hillary gave him a sheepish smile. "Oh, right. The brat thing!" She laughed nervously. "You said, uh, you know, something about *spanking* me or something..."

He nodded. "Bingo. Now that you're obeying me, you'll learn to be respectful." He leaned in so close their knees were touching and she craned her neck to look up to him. "You going to be respectful, Hillary?"

Her eyes widened and she nodded. "Yes," she managed to eke out.

Good. She was exactly where he wanted her, listening to him, completely aware of the fact that she was in trouble, and clearly lapping up every bit of his control over her.

Oh, he was so gonna pay for this.

Grasping her hand again so that she was trotting beside him, he stalked to the office in the back, gave three quick knocks, and waited until he heard Blake's "Come in." Blake, owner and overseer of all that went on in the club, sat at a desk, several dozen monitors mounted on the wall to the side, including one monitor that would show him it was Matteo knocking on the office door. When they entered the office, Matteo pointed to a chair on the side for Hillary to take a seat, and she meekly obeyed.

Blake was in his mid-fifties, a large, stern man with gray hair and dark eyes that missed nothing, a nose that had clearly been broken more than once, and a short, severe goatee. He was dressed in a button-down blue shirt and khakis, and he watched the two of them enter. He sat in front of his computer behind a large, gleaming cherry-wood desk. The office was large but simply furnished, and immaculately clean. He had been into the scene longer than not, and after marrying his long-term submissive several decades prior, opened The Club.

"Matteo," he said in greeting, his voice low and guttural. Matteo nodded back.

"My shift is over for the night," Matteo said. "We had issues in the Red Room, but Slay took over."

Blake nodded. "I know." Of course he did. Everything awry was immediately reported to him via The Club's high-tech communication system, wireless headsets with earpieces that all supervisory staff were required to wear. Blake nodded to the chair in front of him.

"Sit."

Matteo sat as Blake pushed a small tablet in front of him, giving him time to give his report of the night. Matteo knew the routine, and nimbly filled out all the required fields. He was paid amply for the times he was substitute Dungeon Master at The Club, and he took his responsibilities seriously. When he was done, he pushed the tablet back over to Blake. Blake read over the report.

"Good," he muttered. "Thanks for the details. You can go now, and enjoy your evening. However, we need to talk soon," he said. "I've been noticing a pattern of behavior on certain evenings, and piecing things together. Can you come tomorrow afternoon?"

"Yeah," Matteo replied. "I have a morning shift at *Inked*, but will be free after two."

Blake nodded. "Fine. Three good?"

Matteo nodded as he walked to the door, gesturing for Hillary to follow.

"Going to introduce me to your lady friend?" Blake asked, stopping Matteo in his tracks.

Introducing her. It seemed like a big step, somehow. He put a protective arm around Hillary's waist as they turned back around to face Blake.

"Blake, this is Hillary. Hill, Master Blake."

Hillary, clearly intimidated by Blake, nodded and murmured her greeting as Blake fixed his eyes on Matteo.

"Is she the one?"

He heard Hillary's intake of breath as she tensed.

Matteo paused. Blake missed nothing. His stern eyes twinkled as he took the two of them in with a slow nod. "She's the one you saved from that shit storm at Black Box." It was a statement, not a question.

"She is."

Blake nodded knowingly. "I'm aware of what happened." His gaze shifted to Hillary, and his voice softened, a rarity Matteo had never witnessed. "You're safe here," he said. "We ensure shit like that doesn't go down." His eyes went to Matteo. "Still, she's here, she's within arm's reach of you. Yeah?"

Matteo's eyes hardened and he stood straighter. "Hell yeah," he said in a voice just above a growl. Hillary's body softened and she stepped closer to Matteo.

Blake's chin lifted, a subtle acknowledgment that he and Matteo saw eye to eye, and his voice dropped.

"She your sub?" Blake liked to know the relationship status of every one of the people who worked for him.

Matteo paused. How open would they be about their relationship? He looked to Hillary, and he couldn't deny her, couldn't denounce her, and even though he had to keep their relationship from Dom and Heidi, Hillary deserved the recognition. He nodded, eyes meeting Blake's man-to-man.

"Our relationship is not public knowledge," he said. Blake knew Dom frequented The Club but Blake could keep shit tight. He swallowed as he looked at her with pride. "Yeah. She's my submissive."

Hillary was quiet on the way home, and Matteo was aware of what a long evening she'd had. First, the serious courage it took to go and meet Slay to begin with, followed by the roller coaster ride of having Slay not end up being the friggin' dom she went home with, and the confirmation to Blake that she was his sub.

His submissive.

He'd never taken his charge to dom a woman so seriously before. Until Heidi came on the scene, he and Dom had all but made a pact that they were not going to do the 24/7 thing. Then Dom went and hooked up with Heidi, and suddenly... the need to skirt the edge of commitment no longer held the same appeal.

Despite the fact that Hillary and Matteo were both quiet, he didn't find it awkward or uncomfortable. She had a lot on her mind, and so did he, but when his stomach growled, he decided it was time to break the silence.

"You hungry, babe?" he asked, as the stoplight turned green and he accelerated.

"Mmm," she murmured and shrugged, neither a yes nor a no.

"What's 'mmm' mean?" he asked. He gave her a sidelong glance as he drove, noticing her phone was in her hand, and she was texting away. He reached for her phone.

"What?" she asked.

"Hill, when I ask you a question, you're supposed to answer me," he said. "Hand me your phone."

Grumbling, she handed it to him and he placed it face down on the console.

"I didn't know you asked me a question," she protested.

"That's because you weren't listening to me."

"I didn't know I was supposed to be listening to you!"

He flicked on his directional and pulled into a vacant parking lot, cruising to a stop and putting his truck in park. He inhaled and exhaled slowly, turning to face her. She shrugged and smiled sheepishly at him, cringing a bit as he cleared his voice and crossed his arms on his chest.

"Care to repeat that?" he asked sternly.

She squirmed in her seat. "Um. I said I didn't know I was supposed to be listening to you?"

"And what exactly do you think you're supposed to *do* to your dom? Hmm? Any idea?" She sat silently. He narrowed his eyes. "I'm waiting."

"Well... listening would be a good start."

"Damn right, girl. You've already earned yourself a spanking for rolling your eyes at me. Should we compound this?" Her eyes widened and she shook her head.

"No." She laughed nervously. "I think I'm, uh, kinda all set with not compounding *anything* tonight."

Even as he knew she needed him to be consistent and firm, his heart went out to her. It had been a long night for her, and she needed his understanding right now, even if she did need a good spanking to set her to rights.

"Good," he said approvingly. "Now answer my question. Are you hungry?"

She shrugged. "I don't think so. No, not really."

"When was the last time you ate?" he asked.

She bit her lip and seemed to be thinking.

"Well, if you have to think that hard, then it must've been a while."

"Yeah," she said, "It was. I was too nervous before I went to The Club, and I ate a really light breakfast…"

"You girls," he muttered, as he backed out of the parking lot and headed toward his apartment. "Dom has to make Heidi eat all the time. Crazy. How can you forget to *eat?*"

Hillary shrugged. "I have no idea. I do know Heidi got spanked for it last week. She turns into a crazy woman when she doesn't eat."

He snorted. "And what do you turn into?"

She giggled. "A fairy?"

Ah, now they were getting somewhere, if she was able to joke about fairies when she'd done nothing but give him grief about calling her Tinker Bell.

"So when you're displaying particular Tink-like qualities, time to feed you?"

Another laugh. Good, she was starting to lighten up. He wanted her to feel the weight of her impending punishment, but she also needed to trust him, and he'd get a lot further with her if she could lighten up.

"Yep, guess so," she said. "If I start flying and sprinkling you with fairy dust, I need food."

He chuckled. "I was thinking more like if you give me that nose twitch and scowl Tink gives, time to feed you." He paused. *"After* I spank you."

He heard her gasp as he pulled into his parking place.

They didn't speak as he led her up to his apartment. She'd been there so many times, she knew the routine, knew where everything was, and usually made herself immediately at home. But tonight, she shifted on her feet, unusually quiet and nervous and it was obvious to him why. He'd never spanked her, not even a teasing swat, though he'd been sorely tempted on many occasions.

Matteo, however, wasn't nervous. He felt exhilarated, the prelude to taking her in hand when he would remain stern and unyielding. Matteo had administered punishment spankings so many times he'd lost count, on his own terms in his place with whomever he took home, and, on occasion, at The Club when the situation warranted it. He knew the routine, knew how to gauge the emotional reaction and tolerance well, and knew it was important to watch his submissive's cues before, during, and after a discipline session.

In the car, he'd decided he would only use his hand for her first spanking. He had plenty of other implements to choose from, but they could be serious, and she hadn't been spanked very often. He suspected she would be able to take it. Even though she was small, she was strong, but the circumstances didn't require a serious punishment. Considering the effects of making her wait, he weighed the option of going over ground rules before spanking her or getting the punishment over with, but seeing how nervous she was in the car, he decided it would be best to spank her first. She would be on edge and nervous if they discussed things before her punishment. After he spanked her, he'd likely have her undivided attention.

"You thirsty?" he asked, and she shook her head, perched nervously on the arm of his couch.

"I'll cook us dinner after we take care of business," he said nonchalantly, watching her chest rise as she inhaled, and her hands twisting in her lap. "Hand me your coat and bag, and take a few minutes to compose yourself. Then go in my bedroom and I want you standing in the corner when I come in."

Her eyes widened. She hadn't expected that instruction. But it was a useful tool he liked to use, and it would humble her, but also get her focused on her place, and what was to come.

"You want me in the *corner*?" she asked incredulously.

He nodded, leaning up against the counter in the kitchen so that he was facing her, arms crossed.

"Yep. That's what I said."

She frowned and seemed to be warring with herself, trying to decide if she should listen to him or not. He gave her a few seconds to process before he uncrossed his arms, pushed himself off the counter, and took a step toward her, prepared to *take* her to the corner with a sharp swat to her ass if she didn't move. She jumped off the couch and ran to his room, and he shook his head.

Oh, it would be *so* fun to tame Tinker Bell.

When he entered the bedroom a few minutes later, she stood straighter. Her little hands were clasped behind her back, and her chin was lifted – in defiance? Or an act of bravery? He would know shortly. His room was small and clean. A king-sized bed stood in the center up against the wall, a small brown dresser flanked the wall to the right, and the door to the bathroom was next to the dresser. Atop the dresser he had a small basket where he kept his loose change, keys, and shit like that. A laundry basket in the shape of a basketball hoop stood at the foot of his bed, and above his dresser, two small cases with baseballs autographed by various members of the Boston Red Sox.

His tools were all in the little table next to the bed, but he wouldn't be needing any of them tonight. He sat on the edge of the bed and watched as she shifted nervously from one foot to another. He waited a few beats before he called her to him.

"Come here, Hillary." His voice was low and commanding. It was rare he called her by her full name. He needed her to know that yes, he could be her buddy and her friend. Sure, they would drink beer and hang out, and he'd help her pick out those earrings she needed for the wedding. He'd even go with her when she needed to see the new vampire movie but was too scared to go alone, and he'd crack funny jokes and swipe the fries off her plate at Roadhouse. But if he was going to be her dom, she would have to think about how she behaved.

Hillary shuffled over until she stood between his legs. Her eyes were bright and her hands shook when he took them in his.

"You nervous, babe?" he asked softly. A little nerves would go a long way when he was to punish her, but he didn't want her to truly fear him.

She nodded and swallowed. "Yes, sir," she whispered.

It felt nice to hear her say that. He closed his eyes briefly, momentarily taken aback by the power of what was happening between them—Hillary standing before him, trusting and prepared to submit, the erotic charge of her submission making him grow hard before he even took her over his knee. She *needed* this from him. She needed to know he cared enough about her that he would expect her to obey him, that he would take care of her needs and teach her to do as he said. And he realized the taste of her obedience made him want more, her submission satisfying a hunger he couldn't control.

But he could only meet her needs as her dominant if she obeyed him first.

He continued to hold her hands in his.

"You don't have to be nervous about this, honey," he said gently. "If I'm going to be your dom, you'll have to learn to obey me. But I will never take you further than you need to go." Tears came to her eyes as she nodded.

He held her eyes for a moment—those pretty eyes were so fetching and vivacious, so trusting. He nodded. Now was the time. His eyes roamed her body and she shifted under his gaze as if it contained a palpable heat. She was wearing a lilac dress that came together at her waist, some kind of a wrap thing that looked thin. He preferred to spank bare skin, but didn't want her to freak out. He could almost hear her wonder... would he make her remove her dress?

"Lie over my lap," he ordered, releasing her hands and patting his lap.

He heard her inhale as she gently laid her little torso against his knee, her legs dangling behind her. He inhaled. God, she was hot. It would be hard to keep his head in the game and stay focused on making sure she learned her lesson.

"Why am I spanking you, Hillary?" he asked sternly.

She wriggled on his lap, and he was so hard it was painful. "I... rolled my eyes and talked back to you!" she said in a rush of words, her hair falling in her face as he held her over his lap.

"Place your hands flat on the floor in front of you," he commanded. "That's right. I'm *not* going to put up with you giving me lip or being rude. Understood?"

Her "yes, sir," was barely audible. Without further ado, he raised his hand and brought it down with a resounding *slap!* She inhaled as he lifted his hand and gave her another sharp swat. His hands were big and she was much smaller than he was, but still, he got the distinct impression he was not really getting through to her. Was he spanking hard enough? He gave her six sharp swats and paused, his hand resting on her bottom.

"Are you done?" she asked, and his suspicions were confirmed—she seemed frustrated, angry even, her attitude practically begging him to take her in hand.

"Stand up," he commanded. She obeyed, her eyes flashing at him, her lips pursed in a scowl. At times, giving a submissive a wimpy spanking was almost worse than none at all. It would be a tease, barely scratching the surface of what they really needed.

But could she take more—a paddle, a cane, or his belt? And shit, if he stripped her down to her bare skin... oh, God, he'd never be able to keep his hands to himself. He was already barely holding himself together. He'd let her keep her panties, but she had to lose the dress.

"Now that you're warmed up, that's gotta come off," he growled, sterner than before, her defiant glare goading him as he jerked a thumb at her dress. She exhaled, her little fingers nimbly going to the hem of her dress, and it took every bit of self-control he had to keep himself under control as she shimmied the dress up over her hips.

"Oh God," he said, half curse, half pleading, as she stepped toward him.

She was wearing a fucking *thong*.

He couldn't trust himself to speak anymore, so instead he reached for her wrist and pulled her over to him, bodily lifting her up and placing her gently but firmly back over his knee.

"Ten for the eye roll, and five more for sassing me," he said.

The thin stripe of sheer pink fabric on her ass was just about the sexiest thing he'd ever laid eyes on, but he plowed on, determined to do what he'd set out to do.

He lifted his hand and brought it down sharply, cupped just enough that when he connected with her bare skin she arched her back and swore. He felt pleased, knowing he was finally getting somewhere with her. Turned out Hillary's tolerance was higher than he'd anticipated.

"You'll behave yourself," he growled. *Swat!* "And watch how you speak to me." *Swat!* He rained swats on her backside, pleased to see her turning a bright shade of red as she wriggled and squirmed as he spanked her soundly.

"Are you going to obey me?" he asked with another sharp swat.

"Yes!" she said, her voice strangely thick and shaky.

"Will I have to do this again anytime soon?" he asked again with another stinging swat.

"No, sir," she said, and her voice was barely audible this time.

She lay limply over his lap. He knew he hadn't overdone it. Then why was she sniffling, her hands covering her face?

He lifted her up into his arms and held her.

"You okay, baby?" he asked, his instinct to soothe and protect kicking in. She sniffled.

"Oh my God, I needed that," she sniffled. "I—*so*—needed that."

He reached his thumbs out, brushing the tears from her cheeks, and he couldn't stop himself. He needed to comfort her. He needed to soothe her tears. Before he could think too hard about what he was doing and his conscience pricked him, he bent his head to hers and brushed her lips with his. Her body arched, reaching for him, her fingers grasping his neck and holding on. As he opened his mouth, he took her more firmly in his arms, and her whole body rose to meet his. She moaned as he kissed her harder.

No sex!

Swearing silently to himself, he finally pulled away and her head fell on his chest. He groaned, partly from desire, but partly from wanting to kick his own ass.

Chapter 5

Hillary mechanically moved pastries from a pink cardboard bakery box onto a large serving platter on the food table, while trying to pretend she wasn't acutely conscious of Matteo leaning against the mantle on the far side of the living room, looking uncharacteristically brooding and grim as he chatted with Paul.

It wasn't *fair* that someone could be that handsome, that sexy, and that *distracting.* She grabbed viciously at a cannoli with her tongs.

She had a *job* to do today—hosting a wedding shower for forty of Heidi and Dom's closest friends and family in her small apartment was no mean feat, even though the food had come from *Cara* and the desserts from *DiMarino's*, the famous North End dessert cafe where Paul's boyfriend John was head pastry chef. Having both of her parents in one space was like being a spectator at an armed standoff—perilous at the best of times. Trying to keep anyone from figuring out that she and Matteo were anything but friends made it doubly difficult. And her feet, in the cute, leopard-print kitten heels that Heidi had given her, were absolutely on fire from standing up all afternoon.

Plus, she had her own special set of rules she had to follow—rules that Matteo had explicitly laid out when he arrived at her apartment earlier that morning under the pretense of helping her set up for the party. Eat something healthy. Don't drink without permission. Come to him if she felt overwhelmed by her hostessing duties. If she didn't follow *those*, he'd be disappointed and she'd end up over his knee. *Again*. She needed to get her head in the game.

And *still*, all she could think of was the way his broad, callused hand felt as it spread across her back when she was over his knee, and how deep and hungry his voice was when he demanded, "Why am I spanking you, Hillary?"

She let out a deep, shuddering breath, and smiled politely at Dom's former secretary, Louisa, who was filling a plate with food.

Focus, Hillary. You don't want another spanking.

Except… she kinda did.

Because when Matteo was spanking her, as he'd done several times over the two weeks that she'd been his submissive, she didn't worry about what he was thinking, or jealously obsess about what he was doing on the nights he spent at The Club. She didn't wonder whether he was getting tired of her, or regretting his impulsive decision to help her. She knew, in those moments, that his focus was entirely on her and the connection between them was real. The rest of the time, well…

She'd thought she was ready for what life would be like with Matteo as her dominant, but she'd been utterly unprepared for how amazing and frustrating and arousing and *confusing* it would be.

Amazing, because *holy shit*, finally she had someone to give her the rules and structure that she needed. She was writing more—and the sex scenes were finally flowing. She was taking better care of herself, and feeling more confident in herself than she had ever been, simply because Matt helped her define and achieve her goals, and gave her very real consequences when she let herself get distracted.

But it was frustrating, too, because it felt like something was missing—something *besides* the sex, which was a glaring, obvious omission right there. There was a distance between them that felt horribly wrong... Except for that one moment, two weeks ago, when he'd kissed her.

Hillary pressed her lips together, remembering the weight of his lips as they'd claimed hers, the feel of his tongue sliding against hers... It had only been a simple kiss. But it had felt like *everything*.

Until he'd pulled away and *apologized*, for God's sake. "I won't let this happen again, Hillary. You're important to me, and I don't want either of us to get confused about what's going on here. I'm your dominant, but we stay platonic for as long as this lasts."

Which was where the *confusing* part began, because sometimes Matt looked at her with undisguised heat in his eyes, heat that kindled an answering flame deep in her belly. And she knew he got off on dominating her. So what the hell was the problem?

And just how long *would* this last? Because with every day that passed, she realized that she didn't simply need a dominant.

She needed Matteo.

"Oh. My. God. This stuff is *disgusting*!" squealed a voice at Hillary's elbow.

Hillary took a deep breath and wrenched her attention away from Matteo. She glanced down to find Tony's girlfriend Valerie leaning over the table, scowling.

"Something wrong, Val?"

Val rolled her eyes and straightened, her four-inch stilettos allowing her to gaze down at Hillary. She shook her long, honey-blonde hair back from her face and sniffed condescendingly.

"*Yes*. I specifically told Tony that there had to be something *decent* to eat at this party, and what does he do? Baked ziti and fucking chocolate, as far as the eye can see! Heidi might not care what her ass looks like now that she's got Dom locked in, but the rest of us still have to put some effort into our appearance!"

Hillary's fingers flexed around the tongs in her hand, and she forced them to loosen.

I will not ruin my sister's bridal shower. I will not murder one of the bridesmaids in the middle of my living room.

But, *God*, this woman was asking for it.

"Tony made baked ziti and chocolate-dipped cannoli for Heidi at their first family dinner," Hillary told Val with a forced smile. "So she specifically requested that he make it today."

"Right, and everything is all about *Heidi*, hmm? Well, good for her. But we'll see how long *that* lasts," Val scoffed.

Hillary turned to fully face Val. "What's that supposed to mean?"

Val shrugged innocently. "Well, Dom isn't exactly known for being faithful, that's all. I mean, I give your sister bonus points for getting him to propose—I'm sure plenty of women have tried and failed. But really, how long do you expect that he's going to stay with her? She's a sweet girl, but she can't keep a man like Dom entertained for long."

Fury exploded in Hillary's stomach and she could feel her face flushing. That *bitch*. Submissive, Hillary might be, but *no one* was allowed to say shit about her sister. She took a threatening step forward.

"Hillary, dear!" Louisa walked over and laid a hand on Hillary's arm. "You don't have any seltzer, do you? I'm afraid someone spilled some red wine on the tablecloth and—"

"Yes!" Hillary said, seizing on the opportunity. "*Yes*. We have some. In the kitchen. Val and I will go and get it. Be right back."

"What? But, I don't—" Val protested.

"Oh, but you *do*!" Hillary said. "I know you'd *love* to be helpful."

Val opened her mouth to protest, then looked at Hillary's face and seemed to think better of it.

"Fine. Whatever," she agreed, rolling her eyes again and stalking towards the kitchen.

Hillary marched grimly behind her.

Once they reached the thankfully unoccupied kitchen, Val rounded on her.

"What's your problem?" she asked, flipping her blonde waves once more so they fell artfully down her back.

"My *problem* is that *you* are out of control and need to adjust your attitude!" Hillary whispered angrily, not wanting Heidi or anyone else to overhear them.

Val rolled her eyes. "I only speak the truth. It's not my fault that you don't want to hear—"

"No!" Hillary slammed the pastry box down on the counter and took a step closer to Val. "You speak the most fucked up lies I have ever heard. You're spiteful. You're selfish. You're jealous. And Heidi is too nice a person to tell you that, but I am *not*."

Val narrowed her eyes. "You think that just because you're Heidi's sister that you're some kind of princess? You twirl your hair and Dom gives you Heidi's old apartment. You bat your eyelashes and Tony gives you a job. You say the word and Matteo runs to do your bidding? Well, I don't jump just because you say so!"

Hillary shook her head. "That's pathetic. Do you even hear yourself? All you think about when you interact with someone is what they can do for you."

Val flushed red. "Fuck you. I'm good to Tony. I do—"

Hillary held up a hand to stop her. "I really don't want to know *anything* about you and Tony. I just want you to understand that if I hear, directly or indirectly, that you have spoken *one word* about my sister or Dom, I will slap you myself. Do you understand?"

Val glanced nervously at Hillary's hand, and Hillary realized that she'd been brandishing her tongs like a weapon. She quickly set them down on the counter next to the box.

Oops.

Val swallowed and nodded. "Whatever. Fine."

Hillary nodded once. "Want to do a good deed, then?" She opened the pantry cabinet and took out a bottle of seltzer and a rag.

Val rolled her eyes and stalked out.

"Yep. Didn't think so," Hillary said with a sigh.

She leaned against the counter for a moment, looking down at her adorable shoes with loathing. Why couldn't they make shoes that were cute *and* comfortable? The upside of hosting the party, though, was that her entire shoe collection was just down the hall.

She left the rag and seltzer on the counter and detoured down the short hallway to her room. Inside, it was blessedly calm and quiet. She wished she could grab Matteo and hide away in here for an hour. Or ten.

Later, she told herself.

She kicked off her shoes and opened the closet door wide. Flip-flops would probably not be appropriate, right? She settled on a pair of black backless flats and had just slipped her feet into them when the door to her room opened and then shut.

"All right, what gives, Matt?" It was Dom's voice, deep like Matteo's but raspier. "You can't give me a vague-ass warning like 'Stay away from The Club' without giving me the details, brother."

She heard Matteo sigh.

"You want to get into this here and now? Fine. But what I'm about to tell you isn't public knowledge. I don't need anyone else catching wind and freaking out," Matteo warned.

Shit… The closet door hid her from sight and they didn't know she was there. She took a breath to announce her presence, when Dom spoke again.

"If fucking Marauder is making trouble again, I think *everyone* should know."

That name froze Hillary to the spot, a blend of anger and terror paralyzing her. Marauder was back? She gripped the doorframe behind her for support.

"Nah. It's not like last time, Dom. It's not random. At least, not that I can tell. If he's still doing what he did to Hillary, luring random girls to Black Box or some other club, he's operating *way* under the radar."

God, the idea of that guy on the loose, preying on some other girl who was curious about BDSM made her physically ill. If he was still active, why hadn't Matteo told her? Why was Matt hiding information? She needed to know this stuff!

"A tiger doesn't change his stripes," Dom warned. "He's a sick piece of shit, and if he did it once, you know he's doing it again."

"Yeah," Matteo admitted. "Probably. And it pisses me off that we don't have enough proof to get him locked away. But that's not what I'm worried about right now."

"Talk," Dom said. She could picture him with his arms folded across his chest.

"So... you know The Club is a fairly tame place," Matt began.

Dom made a noise of disagreement.

"Dom, you've been to Black Box. You know what I'm talking about. At The Club, we don't do public sex. We don't do blood or fluids or any of that shit. We don't tolerate anything that's not safe, sane, and *consensual*."

If only Hillary had known the difference last spring. She pressed a hand to her churning stomach.

"I get you," Dom agreed. "And everyone who goes there knows that."

"Right. We don't get a lot of shit about enforcing those rules because people who are interested in the hardcore kink head to

Black Box, or that dungeon place up on the North Shore, or that other place down the Cape. We haven't had to be that vigilant about who can join—the whole point is to be open for people who are curious about the lifestyle. But suddenly, a few weeks ago, we started having issues every fucking night."

"Like what?"

"Like a domme doing fucking *knife play* in the Lower Hall. Like a submissive being forcibly gagged by a dominant against her will. Like *another* submissive getting high as a fucking kite in the bathroom because someone gave him drugs that were supposed to be an herbal supplement to *enhance his experience*."

"All this shit is from new members?" Dom asked. "Then *ban* their asses. Problem solved."

"Now, why didn't I think of that?" Matteo said scathingly. "It's not that easy, Dom. The sub who was drugged can't ID the person who gave him the drugs, and he didn't think he was doing anything wrong because he thought he was taking an herbal supplement—a *vitamin*."

Hillary could almost hear Matteo rolling his eyes.

"Not to mention, the guy is Gigi's sub," Matteo continued.

She heard Dom suck in a breath.

"Exactly. Gigi is one of the first members of the fucking place. Blake respects the hell out of her. He's not going to kick her out, and he's gonna think long and hard before he bans her sub. Gigi was absolutely fucking *livid* about the whole experience and is complaining to anyone who will listen that her sub is a victim."

"Shit," Dom said.

"Fucking PR nightmare," Matteo agreed. "And it goes deeper than that."

She heard a thump and peeked through the gap between the closet door and the doorframe to see Matteo leaning heavily against the wall, running a hand over his hair.

"The other night, there was an incident in the Red Room. A

dom was caning a submissive, Laurie, who'd agreed to be part of a scene... and then continued to cane her even after she was *screaming* 'Red'."

Hillary was shocked. Everyone knew that 'Red' was the universal safe word. The dominant should've stopped immediately, unless he was an asshole like Marauder.

"What the fuck?" Dom breathed.

"Yeah, Slay hauled the guy into Blake's office and asked him that very question. And the guy tells Blake, 'I was just doing what your email said!' Apparently, this guy got an email *from Blake* that said they were *suspending consent* in that room for that night."

"*Suspending consent*? And he believed it?" Dom asked skeptically.

"Yep. I mean, you know there are a few girls who *do* get off on that shit, even though it's not allowed at The Club. And God knows, there are plenty of guys who *wanna* believe that *all* girls get off on that shit. So, this guy thinks he's doing what the girl wants, right? He's giving it to her good."

"Christ," Dom said.

"Exactly," Matteo agreed. "Wanna know the kicker? The guy was Manny."

"Manny?" Dom repeated blankly. "The Hawaiian guy? Jesus, he's been there for years. Even before *we* started going!"

"Well, before *you* started going, but yeah. Fucking *years*. And the email looked legit, like one of those advertising emails the club sends out when they're having a special demonstration or something. I've gotta say, if I didn't know Blake personally and know he would never condone something like that, I might have believed it."

"Did they report it to the police?"

Matteo snorted. "Yeah, you know how that went, right? They think it's a 'prank'. Laurie didn't press charges. Fortunately, she wasn't badly hurt—at least not *physically*. And after Blake told him the email wasn't real, Manny practically got on his knees to apologize to her, he was so fucking horrified. Laurie forgave him and he's become her personal club bodyguard."

"As he should," Dom said, menace in his voice. "Who believes that shit without verifying with Blake and with the sub herself?"

"Yeah, absolutely, Manny was an idiot. But the fact remains, someone wanted to plant a seed and provoke violence. Blake's wife, she's an IT guru, and she looked into the emails. Doesn't look like they hacked our email servers or member list, which is crucial."

"Thank God. What a shit storm that would be. For all of us," Dom said.

"Truth," Matteo agreed. "But whoever was behind this clearly knows several people close to The Club well enough to have gotten their email addresses in some other way. And they rigged an account that was only a couple of letters off from The Club's real email address. No one would think to check that stuff when reading an email."

"Did Blake's wife trace the email?"

"Yup. She did some stuff that was, ah, *not strictly legal*, and managed to find a connection between this email and one of Marauder's old accounts."

Marauder. *God*. Hillary gripped the doorframe more tightly.

"Meaning this shit is targeted," Dom concluded.

Targeted? What did that mean?

"That's the conclusion I came to. Blake wants me to work with Slay and a couple of other guys—Thorn, maybe Charlie," Matteo told him.

"Slay, Thorn, and Charlie don't work for The Club," Dom observed.

"I know. Blake and I think it's better that way," Matt replied. "We need guys who are dependable but aren't known to be affiliated with us—they'll hear things we won't. Slay, especially, since he's working at Black Box and Marauder may have friends there. But it's gonna take a while. The asshole is smarter this time around, and that means he's more dangerous."

Hillary personally felt he'd been dangerous enough *before*.

Dom nodded. "And in the meantime…"

"In the meantime, we've gotta be extra vigilant," Matteo said. "Don't go near The Club. Don't let Heidi near it. And keep your eyes open."

"Done," Dom said. "You'll let me know if you need help." It was a statement, not a question.

"Dom?" Heidi's calm voice came from outside the bedroom door, accompanied by a soft knock. "Sorry to interrupt, honey, but it's almost time to open gifts."

Crap. The gifts! Hillary should be out there, ready to write things down and do her bridesmaid duty! How would she get out of here without being seen?

Hillary heard Dom open the bedroom door, and saw him smile when her sister appeared in the doorway.

"What's going on, boys?" Heidi asked. Her tone was light, but Hillary could see that she looked a little worried.

She didn't know the half of it.

"Just secret Angelico stuff," Matteo told her with a wink.

Heidi snickered, and Dom wrapped his arm around her shoulders, pulling her into his side.

"Oh, really? Figuring out how to save the world?" she asked Matteo.

"You know it, Heids," Matteo told her. "We'd tell you, but then we'd have to kill you. Or Dom would have to spank you, at the very least."

Dom cuffed Matteo lightly on the back of the head, as Heidi blushed and Matteo chuckled.

"A few more weeks and *you'll* get to know all the secret Angelico stuff," Dom reminded Heidi. He lifted his free hand and stroked her cheek. "Since you'll *be* an Angelico." The note of pride in his voice was unmistakable, and it hit Hillary hard. *I want that.*

"You lovebirds hurry and open your gifts now," Matteo told them, ushering them out the door. "Can't wait to see how you like my present."

"Gift card for Roadhouse burgers?" Dom asked wryly.

"Better. His and hers thongs," Matteo said, ducking when Dom tried to cuff him again.

Dom shook his head and led a giggling Heidi down the hall.

Hillary tensed, waiting for the sound of the door closing. If she ducked into the bathroom, she could tell everyone she…

"You can come out now." Matteo's voice was very stern and very, *very* displeased.

Oh. Shit.

Hillary closed her eyes and prayed for instant invisibility, the way she had when she was six years old. It worked about as well as it ever had.

"I said come out," Matteo said. He shut the bedroom door firmly. "I meant *now*. You don't want to keep me waiting."

Hillary swallowed and stepped away from the closet.

Matteo was standing in front of the door, his hands folded across his chest and his eyes blazing.

"Eavesdropping?" he asked.

"I didn't mean to!" Hillary said quickly, clutching her skirt nervously in her hands. "I was getting new shoes, and then you came in, and I was going to come out, and then you started talking and I… I… I…"

Matteo raised one eyebrow. "You done?"

"Well, you weren't going to *tell* me!" she accused. "I *had* to listen. I heard everything you said, and clearly you've known about this for a while, but you didn't say a word. How can I trust you if you don't tell me things? Especially when those things concern me?"

Matteo stiffened. His eyes went cold, and he regarded her

silently. She hadn't thought he could look more frightening than he did when he was chastising her, but this silence was far, *far* worse.

"Well! Say something! I'm right, aren't I?" she goaded, desperate for him to speak.

His jaw worked back and forth, and when he finally spoke, his voice was hard and wintry.

"We're not going to do this now, Hillary. I'm too angry and you're needed out there for the gift opening."

That voice. She'd never heard him speak that way before. She'd heard him playful and serious and angry and wry, but never so cold, so disconnected. For the first time, Hillary felt real fear. Was this the end? Had she screwed up so badly that he was going to end things between them?

"I'm sorry. I'm sorry, Matteo," she whispered, wilting.

"Later," he gritted out. He reached out and opened the door.

"But, I..." Hillary began. She was desperate for just the tiniest bit of reassurance, to know that she hadn't spoiled this permanently.

"For God's sake, Hillary, *what did I say?*" he whispered furiously.

Hillary swallowed and nodded, brushing past him and down the hall.

Oh, God. What had she done?

The opening of the gifts passed in a blur. Hillary dutifully oohed and ahhed at sets of silverware and china, nodded over bed linens and towels, and organized the presents into piles for Dom and his brothers to transport to his apartment later. But when it was over, she couldn't remember a single item Heidi had opened. Her stomach was in knots, and she knew her smile was forced.

While the rest of the guests milled around chatting with Dom and Heidi, Hillary excused herself. She belatedly went to grab the seltzer and rag, and attacked the wine stain on the tablecloth.

The red blotch wouldn't budge.

Ruined. Just like every damn thing.

She felt tears prick her eyes and she walked quickly to the kitchen before anyone noticed.

Okay. All right. She grabbed the edge of the sink and took a breath to calm herself. She would talk to Matteo. She would plead with him for one more chance. She would be *so*, so good from now on.

Yes, he'd had to spank her a few times over the past few weeks, but he'd assured her that was normal at the beginning. "You'll come to understand my expectations," he'd told her. She'd been excited at the time, allowing herself to imagine a future where she would know him that well, when she and Matteo would have what Heidi and Dom had.

But those had been minor offenses—forgetting to eat breakfast, forgetting to check her speed when driving. She hadn't *directly argued* with him.

Had Matteo decided she was more trouble than she was worth now?

"Oh, Hillie! Good! I found you!"

Hillary whirled around to see her mother striding purposefully into the kitchen, wavy auburn hair flying behind her, colorful peasant skirt swishing, and beaded bracelets clinking merrily.

Her mother vibrated with suppressed energy—ironic, since Frances Morrow espoused a million different homeopathic ways to reduce stress and align her chakras—and at the moment, all of that energy was fixated directly on Hillary.

What have I done to deserve this right now? Hillary begged the Universe. The Universe didn't reply.

Frances grabbed Hillary's hands so tightly that Hillary felt her joints pop.

"I overheard Matteo saying the most *ridiculous* thing to Heidi's friend John, and I just *knew* it couldn't be true," she said, forcing a laugh. "Because I know I raised my girls to *abhor* the patriarchal status quo! I told John right then and there that Matteo was *mistaken*. I mean, my girls know their self-worth lies in their brains and the sanctity of their *life forces*, not in promoting misogynistic sexual *fantasies*! Right? You *do* know that Hillary, *don't* you?"

Hillary felt her eyes widen. What had Matteo been saying? He *couldn't* have been telling anyone about their relationship... Could he? Was he *that* upset?

She took a step back, until her back was pressed against the sink. "Mom, I...I don't—"

"Hillary Annabelle Morrow!" Her father barreled into the kitchen, his white hair mussed and his lined face frowning in confusion. "What's this I'm hearing from your mother?"

Hillary was frozen in horror. Her father had heard, too?

"What the hell did you go to college for, Hillary?" her father demanded. "Why did you work so hard? Why did I help pay for four years at that school, if you were going to throw it all away like this?"

"Dad, I—" Hillary sputtered, her heart racing and her mind blank. How could she possibly explain, how could she make them understand?

"Oh, Charles, how *typical*," her mother said scathingly. "All you're worried about is your *money*. What about Hillary's *soul*?"

"Her *soul*? Forget her *soul*, Frances!" her father bellowed. "What about her *job prospects*?"

Her... *job prospects*?

Wait, what were they talking about?

"Oh, *money* again!" her mother cried. "Who cares if—"

"*I* care, Frances! *I care*! You want her to be independent, right? Well how's she going to do that if she isn't able to support herself because she made stupid choices right out of college?"

Hillary's head was reeling. Beyond her parents' shoulders, she could see that several party guests were standing in the kitchen doorway, watching them.

"Mom, Dad!" she whispered, finally wrenching her hands from her mother's grasp. "Please just calm down. Can we discuss this... whatever this is... *privately*?"

Or *not at all?*

"You want me to calm down? Then tell me what happened to your plan to get a Master's Degree, missy! Hmm?" Her father's face had gone a deep red.

"I don't know what you're talking about! I never said I wasn't," Hillary began, but her mother held out a restraining hand and cut her off.

"Don't you talk to her that way, Charles!" Frances said fiercely, whirling to face Hillary's father. "Just because *you* don't agree with her choices—"

"Mom! Please!" Hillary tried again. Tears of frustration— with Matteo, with her parents, with *herself*—filled her eyes. But her father spoke over her.

"Me? *You* don't agree with her choices any more than I do!" he said, turning to fully face Hillary's mother.

"Well, yes, but at least I am disagreeing for the *right reasons!*" her mother yelled. She was practically bouncing on her tiptoes in agitation.

"Frances, that is the most—"

Hillary shook her head and buried her face in her hands. They'd turned on each other, and now they'd fight *about* her for an hour without listening to her speak. It had been this way for as long as she could remember.

"Enough," Matteo pronounced from the doorway. He didn't need to raise his voice to be heard, or to be obeyed—both of her parents stopped speaking and turned to him.

Hillary lifted her head and stared at him as well... but he didn't look at her.

"Pardon me?" her father challenged.

"I said *enough*," Matteo repeated evenly. "I understand that you're concerned about Hillary, but this isn't the time or place to talk about it."

Her father bristled. "This is a private discussion, Matteo."

"It should be. But isn't," Matteo replied, his voice still calm. "Not when everyone in the living room can hear you."

"Who cares?" her mother demanded, waving a hand dismissively. "Society needs to make room for free discussion—"

"But you're upsetting *Hillary*," Matteo said firmly. "In her own home. In the middle of a party that she spent a great deal of time and effort organizing."

Both of her parents turned to look at her as though they'd never considered that she might be upset. But she couldn't take her eyes off Matteo. He was rescuing her. Again. Even now, even after she'd questioned him and pissed him off, he stood up for her. His green eyes met hers, steady and firm, and he winked.

She swallowed.

The world was suddenly right side up again.

She turned to her parents. Her mother looked guilty and her father bewildered.

"Matteo is absolutely right, guys. I get that you're concerned about my... choices... but this isn't the time or the place."

"But, Hillie," her mother choked out. "Romance novels?"

Romance novels? *Good God.* Was *that* what this was about?

"Mom, have you ever read one?" Hillary demanded.

Her mother shook her head disgustedly and Hillary rolled her eyes.

"They're not about... misogynistic sexual fantasies, or whatever you just said. They're about empowering women to explore their *own* sexual fantasies, and to *break* societal taboos."

Her mother frowned. "But..."

Her father shook his head. "But if you start publishing this... this... *sex* stuff, you'll never be able to get a *real* book published, and you won't be able to find a decent job."

"Dad, these *are* real books. And this *is* a real job... or at least it will be once I'm established. And I don't mind putting the effort in. This is the stuff I want to write."

"You'll starve," her father said baldly.

Matteo shook his head and walked further into the room, stepping around her parents. He leaned back against the counter so his right arm was barely touching her left and she could feel his heat against her. Without conscious thought, she felt her shoulders relax. She hadn't even been aware of how tense she'd been.

"Actually, that's where you're wrong, sir," Matteo told her father. "I've been doing some research, and romance is by far one of the most popular genres in publishing—over a billion dollars in annual sales."

He'd been doing *research*? On *romance novels*? Oh, Matteo.

"Billion? With a 'b'?" her father clarified, clearly impressed.

Matteo nodded.

"Now, granted, there are no guarantees. But that's true for any artist, for anyone who *creates*, right?" Matteo asked her mother. "You have to express what's inside of you, whether or not it's appreciated by the masses."

Frances drew herself up taller and nodded emphatically, staring at Matteo as though he had just revealed the secrets of the universe. "It's true. I've said so, many times."

He was managing them. They were listening to him! Good God, was there anything this man *couldn't* do?

"Hillary is insanely talented," Matteo told them. "And creative."

"But that's just it—she's got such a vivid imagination. I sometimes worry that she's not disciplined enough," her father confessed with a sigh.

"Oh, not at all, sir," Matteo told him with a perfectly straight face. "I guarantee she's well disciplined."

He did *not* just say that.

To her *father*.

Hillary turned her head to stare at him in shock.

"I mean, she has setbacks from time to time, but she's *dedicated*. She doesn't give up." Matteo turned and met her gaze. "So no one should give up on her."

Warmth bloomed in her belly and spread through her chest. He *hadn't* given up on her, on *them*.

"She's working for what she wants," Matteo finished. "I'm proud of her. You should be, too."

They should?

Hillary's father pursed his lips.

"You're right," he told Matteo. "I'm sorry."

"Respectfully, sir, I'm not the one who needs an apology," Matteo replied.

Her father looked startled for a moment, but nodded. He turned to Hillary and smiled.

"I apologize, Hillie. I shouldn't have yelled. I just worry, I guess," he said sheepishly.

Hillary nodded. "But I'm fine, Dad. I promise."

"I guess you are," he agreed, patting her shoulder. But he wasn't done. He turned to her mother and continued, "I'm sorry, Frances. I shouldn't have yelled at you, either."

Frances looked stunned. "I-I...appreciate that," she stammered, blinking up at him.

He smiled down at her. "Come on," he said. And he wrapped an arm around her mother's waist and led her out towards the living room... past Heidi and Dom, who were standing in the doorway.

Heidi's eyes were as wide as Hillary's as she watched their parents walk out together.

"What happened?" she mouthed to Hillary.

Hillary shook her head and shrugged.

Matteo had happened. But she couldn't say that.

Dom and Matteo exchanged a glance, and Dom led Heidi

back out toward the living room, where it sounded like the first guests were taking their leave.

The moment they left, Hillary turned to Matteo and grabbed his arm.

"Oh, God! I was so worried, Matteo!" she confessed. "I thought you were really mad at me!"

Matteo straightened and looked at her seriously.

"Oh, I am," he told her, his voice grave.

"You... are?" she breathed.

"You hid in a closet and listened to a private conversation. Then you implied that you didn't trust me. What do you think?"

Hillary bit her lip. It sounded particularly awful when it said it that way.

"But you stood up for me," she reminded him. "You said that you were proud of me."

"I did. I *am*. And Hillary, I will always stand up for you," he told her, his eyes warm on hers. "But I'm also going to hold you to a high standard. I'm going to expect you to follow rules, and to *trust* me."

Hillary wilted from a combination of shame at her behavior and relief that he still intended to hold her to those standards. "I know. I will, Matt. I *do* trust you."

He nodded.

"And part of that trust means trusting me to tell you *what* you need to know, *when* you need to know it. *My* decision. Not yours."

Crap. He had a point. A good one.

"Okay," she agreed.

"The second the last guest leaves," he told her, his voice a breath of sound as he leaned over to whisper in her ear. "You're mine."

Her heart stuttered. "Yours?"

"Mine," he repeated. "You need to be spanked, Hillary. Thoroughly. And *I* am going to give you what you need."

She swallowed. She felt more aroused than she ever had in

her life, and he wasn't even touching her. God, she wished he would touch her.

"After all," he smirked, as he stepped away from her. "I promised your dad you'd be well-disciplined. And you know I never lie."

"M-maybe you could explain what 'thoroughly' means?" she asked hopefully.

He raised one eyebrow. "And maybe you could work on the *trust*," he suggested.

Right, trust.

"And the rule following," he reminded her.

Shit! The rules he'd given her. She'd been so distracted...

"I... um... I may have forgotten to eat," she admitted.

"Mm-hmm," he said, like this was what he had expected. "So you'd better do something about that. Quickly. And?"

"I didn't drink!" she told him sincerely. "Not a drop."

"I know. And the other?"

The other? Oh.

"I wasn't overwhelmed by hostessing," she said with a shrug. "Not really."

He eyed her skeptically. "Yeah? Because I saw you marching Val in here earlier, Tink, and it looked like you were about to impale her with a set of tongs."

"Oh. That," Hillary said dismissively. "No, that wasn't a big deal. She was being catty and I told her off."

He looked at her a minute, as though judging the truth of her statement, then his expression lightened.

"Awesome," he approved. "Proud of you. Don't take shit from anybody. That's my girl."

He stepped away and grew serious again. "Remember, Hillary," he told her sternly, pointing his finger. "When the last guest leaves."

Then he left her standing in the kitchen, alone, aroused, and feeling like she'd do anything if she could *really* be his girl.

Chapter 6

"You guys, it was so fantastic. Perfect. Amazing! I'm so thankful for everything you did," Heidi gushed, as she pulled the last bit of crepe paper from the dessert table and balled it up in her hand. She turned to face Matteo and Hillary, who were both folding up the gift table to slide back into Hillary's closet. Matteo shrugged. All he'd done was made sure Hillary stayed out of trouble, though really, that was no small feat.

Hillary, on the other hand, had worked her ass off.

"You know Hill's the one who did all the work," he said. "I was more like the gate keeper... bouncer..."

"Taste tester," Hill interrupted, standing up straight and ticking off his various jobs on her little fingers. God, her hands were so sexy. "Pastry sampler. Salsa jar opener. Trash taker outer. Pastry thief..." She turned her back to him with a smirk as she snagged an empty folding chair. He caught himself mid-swing as he was about to land a swat to her ass but, just in time, he swung his hand out and nabbed another chair.

Holy *shit*. Dom and Heidi were still *there*. That was way too close for comfort. He had to get a fucking grip.

Heidi, Dom, Hillary, and Matteo were the only ones left at Hillary's. Even the girls' parents had left, despite their mom's insistence that she help compost food leftovers and separate recyclables from the trash. Matteo had simply put a gentle but firm hand on her shoulder, assured her that he would personally see to the cleanup crew (would he ever!), and ushered her to the door, sweeping the plastic tablecloth and empties into a trash bag the second the door shut behind her. And now, it was time for Heidi and Dom to go.

He had business to attend to, and he didn't want to make Hillary wait any longer. He would forgive her after he'd punished her, and he was eager to put it behind them. Though Matteo knew Hillary hadn't intentionally eavesdropped at first, she had made a mistake by staying and listening when she knew she hadn't been invited to that conversation. It was dishonest and sneaky and yeah, understandable, but still, he wouldn't tolerate dishonesty. If this was gonna work, she would maintain honesty and defer to his authority.

If this was gonna work...

He snapped the chair up harder than necessary as he stalked past Hillary, took the chairs out of her hands, and marched them to the closet himself.

"I could handle them," she protested, and her chin jutted out as she crossed her arms. Matteo paused, turning to her, and made sure Heidi and Dom were well out of earshot when he leaned down to talk to her.

"You've earned yourself a good spanking already," he said. "Really, Hillary? Gonna give me lip now?"

She withered under his gaze. Good. He was *not* gonna put up with this shit. What was her problem, anyway? He had thought they were making headway with this. She hadn't talked back to him in over a week, and had been making good progress with meeting her goals, getting to bed, eating regularly, even writing more. Where was this attitude coming from? The last time he spanked her, she—

It dawned on him as he placed the chairs in the closet.

When *was* the last time he'd spanked her? It had been at least three, maybe four... hell, at least four or five days ago. *Was she getting antsy?* he wondered, as he stacked the chairs and tables in the closet. The last time he'd spanked her, she'd *thanked* him.

"I feel so much better," she'd said. "I really appreciate you doing this for me."

Maybe she needed more from him. Blake had told him on more than one occasion how his wife got ornery and grouchy if he didn't "keep her in her place" with a good spanking regularly. And just the month before, they were out to eat and Heidi had given Dom lip over something—he couldn't remember what at the moment. She'd excused herself and gone to the ladies' room, and Matteo had asked him, "What the hell is her problem tonight?"

Dom had merely shaken his head with a frown and said, "Nothing a good spanking won't cure. She's overdue. I'll set her to rights." He'd paid the bill and was standing, waiting for her when she exited the ladies' room.

And the very next day, Heidi was her normal self again.

Matteo knew how to give, and he knew how to take, and both giving and taking were necessary in his role as dominant. But maybe he had a thing or two to learn about meeting the needs of a submissive.

Matteo had promised Hillary a good spanking when the last guest left, and the last guests were taking their damn time about leaving.

Heidi and Dom needed to go home.

"All right, lovebirds. Been a long night. I'll help you with the gifts, and help Hill with what's left before I head home."

He helped Dom bring the large stacks of gifts to his apartment, and when he came back, the door to Hillary's apartment was left ajar. He frowned. It didn't matter if he'd only stepped away for a minute. If she was alone in the damn apartment, the door was supposed to be fucking locked. He'd gone over this with her repeatedly.

He pushed the door open and entered her apartment. The look on her face clearly reflected that she knew he was angry. Hillary rose to her feet.

"You look mad," she said. "I know I wasn't supposed to be listening. Really, I've been thinking about this, and I'm really sorry, Matteo. I—"

"We'll discuss how sorry you are after I've punished you," he interrupted. In two large strides he reached her sofa, taking her firmly by the hand and lifting her to her feet. Her eyes widened as he marched her over to her door.

"What have I told you about this door when I leave?" he asked.

She gasped. "I forgot to lock it," she whispered.

"Correct. Place both your hands on the door," he ordered. Maybe a few hard swats while she stared at her door would help her remember to click the lock in place when he left.

Her hands trembling, she placed both her hands on the door.

"Stick your butt out."

She obeyed, bending over as her hands stayed on the door. Holding her tiny waist with one hand to stabilize her, he lifted his hand and *smack!* He delivered a few hard, stinging swats. She jumped from the impact but held position. He spun her around and placed a finger under her chin.

"Point made?" he asked. Her eyes were wide and humble as she nodded.

"Yes, sir," she whispered.

"Good. Now we'll deal with the *big* issue, and when I'm done with you, we will put this all behind us." A look of fear crossed her face as she bit her lip.

"Yes, sir," she whispered. He removed his finger and pointed to the hallway where her bedroom was.

"Corner," he ordered. She knew by now that when she was in serious trouble, he expected her standing in the corner waiting for her punishment. It set the tone and humbled her before he spanked her.

"Yes, sir," she whispered again as she fled the room.

Matteo jumped when he heard a knock on her door. Jesus! He peeked through the peephole and saw Heidi standing at the doorway.

Shit!

He opened the door but not all the way, just enough so he could give her a chin lift.

"What's up, Heids?"

"Left my phone," she said sheepishly. "I think it's in Hillary's room, plugged in on her dresser. I'll just run in and—"

"I'll get it," he said, as nonchalantly as possible. "No worries. Dom's waiting. Just a minute."

He left the door open as he walked as quickly as he could to Hillary's room.

Had she heard him? Her face was impassive, and it was impossible to tell. He wouldn't ask. That would be too obvious. If she *did* hear anything, would she tell Dom?

Hillary jumped when he entered the room but kept her nose against the corner. Good girl. He spied Heidi's phone on the dresser, but first, stalked over to where Hillary was standing in the corner. He grabbed her ass, squeezing so hard he knew it would make her squirm, as he whispered in her ear.

"Good girl, standing in the corner like I told you. Your sister forgot her phone. Now you'll stay right here while I give it to her if you know what's good for you." He released her ass and gave her hair a little tug. "Yeah?"

"Yes, sir," she whispered, so low she was barely audible.

Walking over to the dresser, he removed Heidi's phone and

walked back to the door, where Heidi was waiting. She eyed him suspiciously as he approached the door.

"Hill okay?" she asked.

"She's tired," he said. "Needs a little rest. This your phone?"

She nodded. "Thanks so much, Matt," she said, and thank God, she turned and trotted down the hall. He shut and locked the door behind them. Well, if Heidi suspected anything was up, she kept it to herself. Still. *Jesus*.

Matteo turned and faced the bedroom. Before he spanked Hillary, he always made sure he was under control. Anger was understandable, but spanking her when he was not in control of himself was unforgivable. And hell, he was angry. He'd made it clear how he felt about her locking the door, but now he had to address her dishonesty and her lack of trust in him.

Had he done anything deserving of the accusation? He'd ask her, *after* he striped her ass red. It was time she had his belt.

Matteo stalked into her bedroom and noted that she obediently kept her nose in the corner. He stood behind her, crossing his arms on his chest. The past few times he'd had to spank her, he sat on the edge of the bed and beckoned her over to him. This time was more serious, and he had to make that clear.

"Hillary." His deep voice carried across the silence of the room. She knew he only called her by her full name when she was in trouble.

"Yes?" she whispered tentatively, nose still against the wall. He took in what she was wearing—a pale pink dress that clung to her deliciously—as he decided whether or not he'd have her lift her skirt. God, the platonic side of their relationship sucked the big one. Normally, he'd make her remove all her clothing for a punishment this serious, and when he was done, after she'd been thoroughly spanked, he would follow up with claiming her, taking her beneath him on her bed, and—

He closed his eyes and inhaled.

Fucking *hell* it was hard to dom a girl who was so sexy.

"Turn around."

She turned to face him and he grew hard. He could see her hardened nipples through the light fabric of her dress. Was she turned on by having to stand in the corner? Knowing he was going to punish her? The sound of his voice? His power over her?

Or all of the above?

He always lectured her before he spanked her. It was more effective, making sure she knew why she was being punished. Merely punishing her wasn't enough. His job, as her dominant, was not simply to punish but to teach and correct, with his punishment aimed at helping her focus on her own submission, learning to obey, and overcoming the struggles she had. Punishment was payment for a crime, but discipline was administered with a deeper aim. Without the lecture and discussion, he felt as if a spanking was more punishment and less discipline, with discipline aimed primarily at helping her modify her behavior. And that was what this was all about... wasn't it?

A few well-placed words aimed at her heart were more effective than a harsher, more drawn-out spanking would be.

She stood a few feet apart from him, looking up to him as he was taller than she was.

"Is our arrangement based on trust?" he asked. She nodded.

"Yes, sir."

"Then tell me what you did today that violated the trust between us."

She cast her eyes down, but he cleared his throat and her eyes lifted again.

"I... was dishonest," she said. "I didn't tell you I was in the room when you were talking to Dom and I eavesdropped when I shouldn't have."

He nodded. "Go on."

"And then I implied that you... you weren't acting honorably, hiding things from me, and that I didn't trust you."

Matteo felt a sinking in his stomach as she verbalized what she'd done. There was a breach between them, and he needed to punish her to heal that breach. He'd done his damnedest to be dependable, to be good to her, to be consistent and attentive. Hell, he hadn't even taken a girl home from The Club in weeks, and had focused on nothing but Hillary. Did she have no idea how hard it was to keep their relationship platonic?

He nodded curtly, stepped back and gestured toward the bed.

"Tonight, I'm going to teach you how to present for a punishment. Do you know what presenting is, Hillary?"

Her eyes were wide, and her hands shaking...

"No, sir," she whispered.

"Kneel on the bed," he instructed, gesturing. She did, and her dress made it awkward as her legs were close together. Easily solved. "Hike your dress up to your belly."

She obeyed, kneeling on the bed, lifting the hem of her dress so that he could see the curve of her ass. She wore a thin, lace-trimmed pair of nude-colored panties that barely covered her. They would remain. She'd feel his belt easily through the thin fabric.

"Now, chest down on the bed, and hold your arms out straight in front of you," he instructed. He could hear her breathing from where he stood just a few feet apart from her as she obeyed, her knees on the bed, chest down and she stretched her arms in front of her.

"Good girl," he murmured. So beautiful.

He was still pissed she'd been dishonest, but it pleased him to know that she trusted him, not only to teach her how to be a submissive, but also to discipline her. It took serious strength to do that. The mere presentation of her body, his to punish, was already healing the breach of trust between them.

He took a step forward. Placing one hand firmly on her lower back, he pressed gently.

"Arch, baby," he said softly. She obeyed. Stepping back, he took in the scene and wished for a moment he hadn't chosen a presentation position. It was too easy to imagine getting up on the bed himself, taking her from behind, sliding into her after he warmed her ass...

Inhaling, he stepped back, forcing himself to assume the role of disciplinarian.

She needed a spanking.

"You've earned a strapping, Hillary," he announced, and she shifted slightly on the bed. "You'll stay in position as I spank you, and if you get out of position, I'll strap your sit spot. Do you know where your sit spot is?" he asked.

Her cheek was on the mattress as she whispered, "I think so?"

Placing his hand on her bottom, he trailed his hand down until he reached where her ass met her thighs, the tender spot aptly named "the sit spot" because it was the spot she'd feel tingle or burn every time she sat down. Raising his hand, he delivered a sharp swat to the center of her ass. She inhaled but stayed in position. Lowering his hand, he delivered a swat just as sharp to her sit spot. She yelped and jerked up, with a loud, "Ow!"

"Hurts more there, doesn't it?" he asked. She nodded, falling back to the bed and assuming her position again.

"Very much so, sir."

"Do you want to feel my belt there?"

"No, sir! I do not!"

"Then stay in position," he growled, as he backed away and rolled up his sleeves. She inhaled quietly at the sound of his belt being unfastened.

God, he loved using his belt. The feel of the leather in his hands. The way she squirmed at the sound of him pulling it through the loops on his waist. The sound as it whistled in the air. The sharp crack as it landed...

Holding the buckle in one hand, he wrapped his belt around his hand until he'd fashioned a strap. Doubling it over would intensify the pain, and though she needed a good, hard spanking, the tail end of his belt would be sufficient. He stepped back and addressed her.

"First, we'll deal with the eavesdropping. Should you have been honest with me?"

"Yes, sir!" she said, her voice unnaturally high with nerves as she trembled in anticipation of the first blow.

Thwap! His belt zinged through the air and landed.

Zing! Another hard swat. The difficulty of a strapping was making sure the belt didn't land in the same place over and over again, though occasionally he felt it enhanced the punitive effect of a spanking if it *did* land in the same place.

Thwap! Another hard swat, and though she whimpered softly, she stayed in position. Again and again, his belt fell as he continued to strap her soundly. She was ready for more, and it was time he gave her a good, thorough spanking.

For the dishonesty. For not trusting him.

Because she needed it.

Whack! The belt zinged through the air as he continued to rain swats against her raised bottom, one after another until he could see the red of her skin even through her thin panties.

"For being dishonest," he said with another hard swat that had her reeling. She sat up, and he felt a momentary flash of anger as she quickly dropped back to the bed and assumed the position. But it was too late. He'd been very clear that she was expected to maintain her position.

He aimed and let loose several rapid swats to her sit spot. She yelled out, but stayed in position.

"You." *Swat!* "Will." *Thwack!* "Stay." *Swat!* "In position."

"Yes, sir," she hissed, as he continued.

Whack!

"To teach you to trust me."

Swat!

"So you know to obey me."

And finally, a lighter one. *Thwack!*

"And that one's for being *too fucking sexy*."

He dropped his belt. She'd had enough. Looking to see if she was crying, he saw that she wasn't. She exhaled slowly but maintained her position as he placed his hand on her tender bottom. She flinched, but he knew that massaging her would help ease the pain and restore her calm. It was the hardest spanking he'd ever given her, but he knew she'd needed a serious session, and that going too light on her wouldn't have helped a bit.

"C'mere, baby," he murmured, as he climbed on the bed with her and rested against the pillows. She sat up, pulled her dress down, and crawled over to him. As soon as she was within arm's reach, he pulled her to him, nestling her against his chest, and stroking her soft hair.

"You okay?" he asked in a low, soothing voice.

He hadn't always been a fan of aftercare, and often spankings he doled out were for bedroom play and not truly disciplinary. But if Hillary needed him, he *had* to meet her needs. Comforting her after a spanking was difficult. Remaining platonic and chaste was damn near impossible, especially when she was at her most vulnerable, just having presented her ass for discipline, and the mere act of her submitting herself by lying over the bed or his lap was like an aphrodisiac.

Hillary snuggled up on him, but she didn't cry. She inhaled and exhaled in deep, cleansing breaths, and it pleased Matteo to know he'd given her what she needed.

"And I was afraid we were done," she whispered. He sat up straighter, surprised at her admission.

"Done?" he asked.

"Yeah," she said. "Earlier, in the bedroom. You were so angry at me. I thought you didn't want anything to do with me anymore and that we were through."

He sighed. "Hillary, why do we do this?" he asked, his voice gently chiding.

"To... help me?" she asked. "So that I can discover if I really *am* a submissive. And after that, by the way, yes, I totally think I am, in case you were wondering. I mean, I—"

"Woman," he warned.

She giggled. "Yes?"

"Answer the question."

Nodding, she continued. "To help me stay focused and on track. Get my writing in and take care of myself. Give me the structure and discipline I need."

"Exactly. But one of the benefits of this agreement is that we have a tool to resolve conflict. You get me?"

She was quiet for a minute before she answered. "I get you," she whispered.

"I'm not going to *reject* you if you do something you shouldn't," he said. "I'm going to *spank* you."

She nodded thoughtfully. "Clearly," she said, but he could tell she was pleased.

"And then whatever the issue is, the punishment clears the air and we move on. You get me?"

"I do."

He reached a large hand out to her bottom and she winced.

"Sore, honey?"

"Um, yes, sir," she said.

"Good," he said sternly. To his surprise, she laughed, and for the first time in a while, he realized she was laughing freely, unreservedly, as if she were somehow lighter and at ease. He joined her, chuckling as he held her to his chest and ran a hand up and down her back in long, soothing strokes, starting at the top near her shoulders, down, down, past the small of her back, and all the way to her bottom where he delivered a playful pinch.

"Ooooh," she moaned, and to his horror she lifted her leg as if to get away from his pinching, hitching one gorgeous, bare leg with her knee bent, so that she was fairly straddling him.

"Hillary," he groaned. He went to push her knee off of him, but found her bare skin impossibly soft, and *Jesus* she smelled *so good*. Instead of shoving her off, he gently stroked her knee, his thumb massaging her, which elicited a low moan from her.

She could not moan.

No moaning!

Too late. He was already rock hard and struggling to keep his mind where it should be. Then her little hand went out and lay flat on his chest. He lifted her fingers to his lips and kissed. He felt her inhale, and before he knew what he was doing, he'd opened his mouth and lightly nipped her little fingers. Oh, God! She was pushing herself up on his chest, and he lifted her, his mouth crashing on hers as his hands spanned her waist. He shifted her up to him so they were flat against each other, the heat of her body pressed against the hardness of his erection. His tongue plundered her mouth and she shifted her hips against his.

His mind vaguely noted a prick of a conscience before his body took over. With ease, he pushed himself up, pushed her gently off him, tumbled her onto the bed, and straddled her, one arm reaching to lift her to him as his other reached for the silky fabric of her dress. He trailed lazy fingers across her chest until he felt her nipples harden beneath him, and then he pinched, just enough to cause her pelvis to arch into him. Her moan begged him to do it again. He nipped her lip as he pinched her nipples, lifting her body to his as his desire for her mounted.

"Beautiful," he murmured, "Gorgeous. It's not fair how sexy you are," he moaned.

"You think so?" she said, and her voice wavered. "Oh, God, I thought you didn't think so," she said, almost as if to herself.

He wanted to put her right over his knee again. He glared at her, pushing himself up so she could feel the full weight of his eyes narrowed on her.

"You thought *what?*" he asked. His anger was not lost on her, as she shrank beneath him.

"That you didn't find me pretty," she said. "You only kissed me once and then you *apologized* for it, and then you—"

His mouth silenced hers as kissed her hard, one hand on either side of her face as he tried to convey without words just exactly how gorgeous he found her. He wrenched his mouth off hers as he pinned her wrists to her sides and his mouth went to her neck. He kissed, then he lightly nipped the tender skin and she arched her back in pleasure.

"Not *pretty?*" he moaned, as her hips tipped forward and his erection ground against her soft belly. "Not *pretty?*" he repeated as one hand reached and caressed her breasts, begging to touch the bare skin beneath but not willing to break his pact. "I didn't kiss you because you're *too damn pretty* and I'm afraid if I don't hold myself back, I'll do something like this."

He lifted the edge of her dress and his fingers found the soft silk of her panties.

"Oh my God," she moaned as his rough fingers stroked and she ground against him.

"Such a pretty girl," he said. "So beautiful. And you took your spanking bravely, baby." His fingers continued to stroke lazily along the silk edge of her panties, and her head tossed to the side of the pillow as his mouth dropped and he licked her neck. She moaned as he sucked at her naked skin at the same time his fingers stroked, again and again, determined and unapologetic.

"Please," she whispered, and he wasn't sure why she was pleading. Did she want him to stop? Or did she want more? His mouth still on her neck, he lazily trailed his finger to the edge of her panties and felt her hold her breath. Slowly, deliberately, he trailed his fingers on her skin, one teasing finger plunging deep and fondling.

"*Yesss,*" she hissed.

He had his answer. He lifted his mouth to her ear.

"Can you come for me, baby?" he whispered.

"Oh my God, yes," she answered, and he lifted his mouth to hers, kissing her as he continued to bring her to climax.

"Come for me," he ordered, and she did, her hips writhing beneath the strength of his hands as he held her, moans escaping her lips as she came so hard he had to hold her down. *Fuck* if it wasn't the sexiest thing he'd ever seen, Hillary's powerful, uninhibited release. Finally, she sank to the bed and he held her against him.

"Good girl," he crooned. "Good girls deserve rewards," he said with a chuckle.

"I will do whatever you say without question for the rest of my goddamn life," she moaned, one hand over her head, her eyes shut tight.

"The hell you will," he said with a chuckle. "But maybe that'll keep the brat at bay for a day or so."

She opened one eye.

"So. Getting spanked makes me come harder. Duly noted. And if you're really worried about the brat, we can try for round two, just to ensure—"

He flipped her over and spanked her, chuckling as she moaned.

Impossible.

They sat at her dining room table, drinking beer leftover from the party and chips straight out of the bag, dipped in a jar of French onion dip.

"We can't do that again," he said, leaning back in the chair with a sigh.

"No sex," she said, nodding in agreement. "But that wasn't really *sex*, it was—"

"Hillary."

She blinked and bit her lip, giving him a fetching grin. "Yeah?"

"We can't do that again."

She seemed to be warring with herself, but in the end, she sighed. "Fine."

A beep came from the side of the table, and she reached for her phone, tapping on it and frowning. "This is the weirdest thing ever," she said. "Someone's got the wrong number. They keep sending me these messages, and I don't even know who it is."

He was immediately on alert as he lifted his hand and beckoned for her to hand it to him. She shrugged.

"It's not a big deal, Matt, it's just weird."

Scrolling through her messages, he saw this was the second message she'd gotten from the anonymous number in two days. The first was a "hi," which she hadn't replied to. After that a second "Hello."

"People with wrong numbers don't keep pestering," he muttered. "What the hell?"

"It's nothing, Matt," she said, as he replied to the text message.

Wrong number. Please stop messaging.

He dialed the phone number, but it just went to an anonymous voice mail message.

"Please leave your message after the beep."

Frowning, Matteo put the phone down and tapped his fingers on the table.

"How weird," Hillary said as she stood, looking curiously over his shoulder. "There's a gift on the mantle. It must've been one that Dom and Heidi left." She reached for it, but as she did, she froze. She turned to face Matteo, her pretty face paling.

"It has my name on it," she said.

"Hand it to me, Hill," he ordered. She obeyed quickly, passing him the small box covered in shiny red paper.

He flipped it around, looking for a card, but there was none other than a tag that said *Hillary* in bold black lettering. Matteo slid a finger under the fold of paper and tore. Hillary jumped, and he looked up at her in surprise. She was on edge, poor girl.

"Come here, baby," he said. "Sit."

She obeyed, as he continued to open the box. He lifted the lid and when he did, she gasped. Inside, nestled against a bed of white tissue paper, was a pair of silver handcuffs and a black blindfold.

"Is this some kind of sick joke? What the fucking hell?" Matteo muttered, shoving it back in the box as his own phone buzzed. It was a message from Blake.

Shit going down tonight. Keep your girl safe. We'll talk later.

Matteo put his phone down on the counter and scowled.

"Pack your bag. You're coming to my place."

Chapter 7

Hillary twisted her neck back and forth, appraising her appearance in Matteo's bathroom mirror. She sighed. Her skin was pale from too many days stuck indoors, she had circles under her eyes from lack of sleep, her sundress was wrinkled, and her hair, without the aid of her trusty hair products and blow dryer, was a mass of unruly platinum-blonde waves with an inch of auburn roots showing at the top. But it was as good as she was going to get.

Life lesson: When the hot dominant in your life tells you to pack a bag and head to his place, don't start mentally squealing and picking out your sexiest lingerie. Instead, ask the important follow-up questions, like, "How long will I be on lock-down, Matteo?" And, "When should I tell Tony I'll be back to work?" And, "You do have a hairdryer, *right*?"

Why had she assumed that a man who had barely two inches of hair on his head would have a hairdryer?

Why had she assumed that a man so obsessed with her safety that he insisted she routinely lock the door behind her when she went out in the hall to check her mail would be remotely reasonable after she'd received all of those text messages and that... gift?

The blindfold and cuffs had been horrifying. If not for Matteo's constant reminders to focus on her daily rules and to trust him, she would have made herself sick imagining how the gift had gotten to be on her mantle. Had Marauder or one of his friends been inside her apartment, touching her things, looking at her family pictures? She wasn't sure if she felt better or worse once Matteo had tracked down the truth—that a guy claiming to be an old friend of hers had handed it to her dad to bring in.

Marauder had handed it to her *dad*. Had talked to her *dad*. He'd been near her *family*.

Hillary shuddered.

Still, that had been over a week ago, and he hadn't contacted her since. Wasn't it likely that he'd given up? Wasn't it, maybe just *maybe*, time for Matteo to lighten up a little bit? Having Matt or Slay or one of their friends escort her every time she went to Stop and Shop had gotten old. She'd missed so much work that her bank account was crying. It had been nearly impossible to keep her absence a secret from her sister who practically lived *next-freakin'-door*, and, *oh yeah*, her sexy, sweet dominant had been a bossy grump with a perma-frown for *days*.

Definitely no need for the sexy lingerie.

Fortunately, she'd remembered to pack her laptop, otherwise things would have been really desperate. Hillary might not have had any need for lingerie, but she'd managed to channel her sexual frustrations into her writing, and her *characters* had been finding a thousand new and inventive ways to get it on. In fact, her first novel was closing in on a happily-ever-after.

How pathetic was it when you envied fictional characters?

"Tink!" Matteo's impatient voice was accompanied by a brisk knock on the door. "Let's go."

Hillary rolled her eyes and made a face in the mirror. Why

did that imperious tone make her belly flip over in such a good way?

Maybe because he wound you up last Sunday and, no matter how many sex scenes you write, you haven't cooled down?

Last weekend, he'd told her they could never cross the line again, and she'd pretended to agree... She'd been trying to respect his need to keep things platonic, but she didn't understand it. He knew how she felt about him... maybe he wanted to make sure she understood he didn't return those deeper feelings? Or maybe he worried that she was too damaged by what Marauder had done?

He kept telling her that she needed to come to him with her questions and her concerns, but how the heck was she supposed to say, "Why won't you sleep with me?" What if he backed away even further? Still, every time she thought he was relenting, like after that mind-blowing spanking and orgasm last weekend, he pushed her away again. She'd had three sessions over his knee this week, and he'd been extremely focused and attentive each time, but not once had he so much as kissed her afterward.

She threw open the door. Matteo was standing in the doorway, wearing his everyday uniform of jeans, boots, and a tight black t-shirt. Her mouth watered.

"You really don't have to drive me, Matt," she reminded him. "It's just lunch with Heidi at *Cara*. It's a two-minute drive away, and then I'll be under Tony's watchful eye, plus Tess and Nicole will be right there, and I know all of the people in the kitchen. It's like having built-in bodyguards."

Predictably, Matteo scowled.

"We've already had this discussion. What have I told you about arguing with me?"

Hillary stifled a sigh. They'd had this discussion *a lot* in the past two days, and she really ought to know better by now. She cast her eyes down.

"That it's disrespectful. I'm sorry, sir," she said meekly.

"Mm-hmm. Finish getting dressed," he told her.

"I'm finished!" she replied. "Just need to grab my purse." She tried to scoot past him into the hallway, but he wouldn't move.

"*That* is what you're wearing?" he growled, his eyes roving over her.

Hillary looked down at herself. She was wearing a navy blue sundress with spaghetti straps that crossed in the back, and a frilly, A-line skirt that hit her at mid-thigh. Paired with her flat silver sandals, it was perfectly appropriate for the unseasonably hot September day... Wasn't it?

"Um... yes?" she ventured.

"Um... *no*," he said firmly, crossing his arms over his chest. "That looks like the... what do you call it? The thing you wear *under* the dress," he told her. "It's too fucking sexy. Put something else on."

She frowned. "Matt, I don't *have* anything else. This is the only dress I brought with me."

"Are you arguing *again*?" he demanded.

"No! I'm just trying to explain," she told him honestly. "I've worn this before, lots of times, and I..."

She broke off when he took a step forward, crowding her against the wall.

"But I wasn't your dominant *before*, Hillary," he reminded her, his left hand coming up to cup her cheek and hold her in place.

The way he said her name—her full name—in that deep, serious voice made her nipples tighten. She pressed her head and shoulders back against the wall.

"Yes, sir," she breathed.

"Do you see how revealing this is? Hmm?" His right hand traced a line from her throat, across her collarbone, and down. Hillary swallowed.

"Do you see how fucking sexy you are?" he demanded.

God, what had gotten into him? *Please don't stop*, she begged with her mind.

His eyes were focused on his index finger as it dipped just below the edge of her dress and traced a path across the swell of her breast.

"Do you see how just the slightest touch," he whispered, his words fanning heat across her sensitive skin, "could make this happen?" He hooked his finger around one spaghetti strap and slid it down her shoulder. "Do you want this to happen, Hillary?"

Oh. Yes.

Hillary's breath was choppy and her heart was racing. Her limbs were frozen, not wanting to move an inch lest she should break whatever spell had come over him, but his focus never wavered. With the same slow deliberation, his finger traced back across her chest and gave her other strap the same treatment.

Her dress fell two inches, almost baring her nipples. He swallowed, his gaze transfixed on her breasts.

Hillary purposely took a deep breath as he tugged... and the dress fell to her waist.

"God," he breathed, echoing her thoughts.

With the same finger, he lightly traced a circle around one hardened nipple and watched it tighten further.

Hillary moaned.

"You're so perfect," he told her.

And then he lowered his head.

With his tongue, he traced the same path his finger had taken, around and around, before finally drawing her nipple into his mouth and biting down gently.

"Ah!" she cried. "*Please*, Matteo!"

"Please?" he repeated, sliding his tongue to her other breast. "Please what, baby? Do you want this?"

He captured her nipple with his lips and sucked deeply. Hillary felt an answering pulse low in her belly.

"Yesss," she gasped.

"What do you need, baby, hmm?" His left hand moved down

from her face to play with her other breast, and Hillary was too adrift in sensation to speak.

"Tell me!" he demanded softly.

Her hips lifted involuntarily. He moved his leg between hers, rubbing against her sensually. "Is this it?"

Hillary whimpered. "Please!" she said again. It seemed to be all she was capable of saying.

"Okay, baby," he soothed her. "I've got you."

He stepped back for a moment, and Hillary almost cried at the loss of friction, but he was back a moment later, on his knees. He lifted her dress and quickly stripped her panties, his big hands holding her steady while his thumbs stroked her inner thighs. She closed her eyes with a low moan.

"Hillary," he growled. Her eyes snapped open.

"Watch me," he commanded.

His compelling green eyes locked on hers, he lifted her left knee to curl around his shoulder, and his mouth dipped between her legs.

Hillary's knee buckled at the rush of sensation, and she cried out. But Matteo's big hands found her hips and held her still while his tongue did wicked, wonderful things, finding and stroking the most sensitive places, until she was mindlessly keening his name.

Then he slipped his fingers inside her, and the pleasure built until it was more than she could bear.

"God, I can't—" she gasped.

"Yes, you can. Take it, baby. You take everything I give you, my good girl," he crooned.

He lifted one hand to torment her aching nipples, and lowered his mouth once more.

Hillary came crying his name, and he eased her through the aftershocks until her body slumped bonelessly against the wall.

He set her leg gently back on the floor, then slowly rose to his feet, pressing tiny, hot, tender kisses against her leg, her stomach, and the swell of each breast. He smoothed the skirt of her dress down her thighs and grasped the straps, which were still hooked around her elbows, to pull the top of the dress back into place.

Hillary stared at him, beyond speech.

His chest heaved and his eyes were wild, but his hands were gentle as they sifted through the hair on both sides of her head, holding her in place.

"Tinker Bell?" he murmured, closing his eyes tightly and resting his forehead on hers.

She swallowed. "Yes?" Oh, gosh. This was it. The moment everything would change.

Her voice was barely a whisper but she was ready to promise him anything, agree to anything he asked.

"Go change your damn dress, baby," he whispered. Then he pressed a firm kiss to her forehead and straightened, taking a deliberate step away from her.

"Better hurry if you don't want to be late," he told her.

Then he strode down the hall toward his living room, leaving Hillary gaping after him.

What. The. *Hell.* Just. Happened?

"Another white sangria, please," Hillary told their waitress. "In the largest cup you can find."

Nicole, who just finished covering the lunch rush, chuckled sympathetically as she wrote the order on her pad. "You've got it, babe. One *vat* of sangria, coming up."

Across the table, Heidi's eyes widened.

Hillary pushed down the niggle of guilt that popped up in her mind. No one had told her not to drink today, and damn but she needed it.

"Um... another cranberry and soda with lime," Heidi told Nicole.

As Nicole nodded and moved away, Heidi leaned forward and tucked a strand of long, brown hair behind her ear. "*Two* sangrias at lunch?" she questioned, a thread of censure in her voice.

Hillary brushed an imaginary speck of lint off the fitted blue t-shirt she'd thrown on, along with a plain black pencil skirt, before rushing out to meet Matteo for an extremely tense and silent ride to the restaurant.

Oh, if Heidi only knew. After the messed up, emotional roller coaster of a morning she'd had, it was a wonder Hillary hadn't been doing shots by 11:00 AM.

She squirmed in her seat as the memory of Matteo's hands on her hips, his green eyes looking up at her, made her belly spasm.

But she couldn't tell Heidi any of that, of course. She couldn't tell Heidi *anything* about her relationship with Matteo. Which was fine, honestly, because what would she have said? "Well, you see, Heidi, Matteo and I are in a D/s relationship, like you and Dom. But don't worry! It's perfectly safe, because our relationship is completely platonic. Well, except for the kissing. And the mind-blowing orgasms. Oh, and the fact that I'm hopelessly in love with him."

Yeah, somehow she felt that wouldn't go over well.

"Well, the sangria here is great," she said instead, picking at her Cobb salad and hoping Heidi would drop it.

Of course, that was too much to hope for.

"Something's going on with you," Heidi accused. Her eyes narrowed and she set her fork down on her own salad plate with a clink.

Hillary sighed. "Not really," she said. "Just the usual—work, writing, watching American Ninja Warrior."

Heidi nodded slowly and, Hillary thought, suspiciously. "So… nothing you want to talk to me about? Nothing you'd like to discuss with your big sister?"

"Uh... no? Nope. Not that I can think of." Hillary forced a smile and changed the subject. "So, what did you decide about the napkins for the wedding? Orange with the white border? Or white with orange?"

Heaven knew, the best way to distract her sister was to bring up the wedding, especially now that it was only days away.

Heidi's eyes widened, as if on cue. "White with orange? That was *never* an option! I picked orange with white. The caterers said it was bold and just perfect for a fall wedding, and I agreed. Why? Do you think white with orange would've looked better?" she demanded.

Hillary felt a momentary pang of remorse. Heidi was uncharacteristically stressed about even the most minor details, and the point of this lunch was to get her mind *off* the last-minute wedding stress, not to make her dwell more.

"No way," Hillary said decisively. "Orange with white was the way to go. Very striking for an autumn wedding."

"Do you think Dom will like it?" Heidi asked. "I mean, I know he doesn't really have a preference about the napkins, for goodness sake, it's just... I want everything to be perfect, you know? *Special*. It's, like, a way to show him how much I love him."

Hillary snorted. She couldn't help herself.

"Heids," she said, reaching across the table to grasp her sister's hand. "It doesn't matter if you have orange napkins or purple plaid napkins or *no napkins at all*. If the guests arrived dressed in togas, the caterers served nothing but French fries, and they played the theme from *Game of Thrones* as you walked down the aisle, I can almost *guarantee* Dom wouldn't notice. And, frankly, I'm pretty sure *Matteo* would think that was the most kick-ass wedding he'd ever been to," she said, making Heidi chuckle. "The point is, as long as you and the priest are there, Dom will be thrilled. That's all he wants."

Heidi's smile was brilliant. "You're right. I know you're right.

I sometimes just can't believe it, you know? I have to pinch myself."

She paused as Nicole came back and set down their drinks.

"I just can't believe that this time last year, I was living in Portland, working sixteen hour days and thinking I was happy. I had no clue," Heidi finished, shaking her head.

Hillary forced a smile. A year ago, Hillary had still been a sweet, innocent senior in college, daydreaming about romance and how great things would be once she got to start her adult life. She'd had no clue, either.

"It'll be that way for you," Heidi predicted. "This time next year, you'll be saying the same thing."

Hillary shook her head and toyed with the rim of her sangria glass—an enormous beer stein, as requested—before taking a large sip.

She couldn't imagine what would be happening this time next year. She couldn't imagine what would be happening with her and Matteo next *week* for goodness sake.

"So, I knocked on your door yesterday and you didn't answer," Heidi said, watching Hillary carefully.

Crap. Hillary had been afraid of that. "Oh?" she said lightly. "I must've been at work."

"At the restaurant? At 8:00 AM?" Heidi asked, grilling her like a *Law and Order* prosecutor who'd gotten a suspicious witness on the stand. *Jeez*.

"Oh, you meant in the *morning*." Hillary tried to shrug casually. "I think that must've been when I ran to the store. You must've just missed me." She quieted her conscience with the knowledge that she wasn't lying, exactly—she *had* run to the store at about that time yesterday. She just hadn't been to her *apartment* at all.

"Do you go to the store *every* morning?" Heidi asked. "Because I knocked on your door the day before, too, and you weren't there."

Hillary widened her eyes. "Well, I can't remember *where* I was Thursday morning. Yeesh. I wasn't aware I'd need an *alibi*. I've been busy."

"And then," Heidi continued as if Hillary hadn't spoken. "I realized I hadn't seen your car all day Thursday."

Hillary narrowed her eyes. Really? "Heids, I appreciate you wanting to keep an eye on me, but I'm an adult—"

Heidi talked over her. "So when I knocked and you didn't answer yesterday, I decided to use my key and let myself in."

Hillary's eyes widened in horror and no small amount of anger. "Are you kidding me? You broke in to my apartment?"

"I was concerned," Heidi defended. "All of this stuff has been happening, and I… I was really worried."

Hillary sighed, her anger evaporating as she heard the tremor of real fear in her sister's voice. "You heard about Marauder?" she asked.

"Wait, *you* heard about Marauder?" Heidi asked. "Because I thought Dom said that he and Matt had decided to shield you from all this, *which I did not agree with*," she added quickly, seeing Hillary's face. "But I knew they had your best interests at heart."

Hillary rolled her eyes. "Yeah, well, I don't think Matteo *intended* to tell me. I just happened to overhear a conversation between him and Dom at your wedding shower," she confessed. "So I kinda figured it out."

Heidi's eyes widened. "Oh, shit."

Hillary nodded. "Mm-hmm. Matt was not pleased."

"That explains a lot," Heidi mumbled, nodding to herself.

"What do you mean?" Hillary asked.

Heidi hesitated, then waved her hand dismissively. "Never mind. Tell me what you heard."

Hillary shrugged and told her sister everything she had learned the previous week, including the mysterious appearance of the gift at the shower.

"God, I had no idea he sent you a gift," Heidi breathed, her eyes wide. "That makes it so much creepier."

Hillary nodded. "So, Matteo's been extra vigilant," she told Heidi. "Making sure I get rides wherever I go, asking Tony to give me some time off work, that kind of thing. He's a good guy."

"Of course," Heidi agreed. "Dom's been the same way with me. Especially after all the stuff that happened at The Club the other night, and the flowers."

Hillary frowned. "Flowers? What flowers?"

Heidi's eyes widened. "Oh, damn. You didn't know about the flowers?" She bit her lip as though deciding whether to continue.

"Heidi!" Hillary demanded.

"Fine, fine. Someone sent you flowers the other day, and you didn't answer the bell. The delivery guy didn't want to leave them out in the heat, so he rang our bell to see if he could leave them with us. When Dom saw the card, he called Matteo," Heidi explained. "I don't know what the message was, but they were from... *him*."

Marauder had sent her flowers?

"And no one told me," Hillary said flatly.

"Well, they wanted to protect you, obviously!" Heidi exclaimed. "That's just the way these guys are. You can't stop the sun from shining, and you can't stop an Angelico from protecting the women he loves. And don't be pissy about it, Hillie, because I know you get that."

Hillary blew out a breath. She *was* pissy. In fact, she was furious. How nice for Matteo that he got to make all the decisions —*he* decided what she needed to know and when; *he* decided when he kissed her and when she'd have a freakin' orgasm. It was all so one-sided!

She was supposed to give him her trust, and she wanted to! But was she supposed to trust his *words*, when he told her that their relationship was platonic and their moments of heart-stopping connection could "never happen again"? Or should she trust the heat in his eyes, the absolute focus and devotion she felt when he let himself be with her completely, the way he had this morning? How could she trust him when she didn't understand his motives?

"Don't you ever just want to *scream*?" Hillary demanded. "They can be so high-handed and bossy and *controlled*. Just *once*, I'd like to read his mind, to know what he's *really* thinking."

Heidi smiled triumphantly. "Now we're getting somewhere," she said. "You sound *exactly* like I felt when Dom and I first got together."

Hillary caught herself. Shit! What had she said?

"You ought to know a couple more pieces of information," Heidi told Hillary, sipping her drink calmly. "I've already mostly guessed that you've been staying with Matteo."

Hillary's eyes widened. *Crap.*

Heidi held up a handed and counted off on her fingers. "First, from what I saw in your apartment, you haven't been home in days. Second, he's been chauffeuring you all around town. Third, when I called you to set up this lunch date the other day, I distinctly heard the Sox game in the background—I recognized it well, since it was already playing in my own living room—and Hillie, you don't watch baseball."

Hillary knew how a deer in headlights must feel. Should she deny it?

Heidi seemed to read her mind. "Don't bother denying it. That'll just make me mad," she said.

Hillary sighed.

"The other day, after the shower, I left my phone at your place," Heidi reminded Hillary. "So I came back to get it."

She had? Oh, *right*. She vaguely remembered Matt saying that while she'd been standing in the corner. "Okay," Hillary agreed warily.

Heidi smirked. "Perhaps a *different* person wouldn't have *noticed* the distinct sound of your butt being spanked up against the front door of your apartment, but I know that sound, Hillie."

Hillary felt herself flush bright red. "Oh, God," she moaned, burying her face in her hands.

Heidi giggled. "So, let me ask you again," she said. "Anything you'd like to talk about with your big sister?"

"He—Matteo—he's my…uh. Gosh," she stammered, taking a huge gulp of her fruity drink. "This is harder to talk about than I would have thought."

It was Heidi's turn to reach across the table and take Hillary's hand.

"He's your dominant," Heidi guessed.

Hillary watched her warily, but didn't deny it.

Heidi nodded as if this were confirmation. "I figured. Dom is gonna lose his mind," she said, snickering and shaking her head.

Hillary's eyes widened. "You can't tell him! Heidi, you can't! It'll ruin everything! Matteo said no one could know!"

Heidi's eyes grew wary. "I don't keep things from Dom, Hillie. I *can't*. You know that."

"But… what if you just *suspected* something, and didn't know for sure. Are you required to share every *suspicion* with him?"

Heidi looked skeptical. "I guess not," she said slowly.

"So… let's say there was this hypothetical case," Hillary said.

"Oh, Lord," Heidi groaned.

"Just listen. Let's say that a person, a *submissive* person, thought she really wanted to find a dominant. Okay?"

"Okaaay," Heidi agreed warily.

"And let's say that a, um, friend who was a dominant offered to help that submissive in her search."

Heidi snorted. "Right! Because there's no conflict of interest *there*!"

Hillary frowned. "What?"

Heidi waved a hand for her to continue.

"Okay, well let's say that friend wasn't able to help the submissive and offered to dom her himself..."

Heidi smiled. "Uh-huh. That would not surprise me in the slightest."

"Platonically," Hillary finished.

Heidi choked on a sip of her drink. "Platonically?"

Hillary nodded.

Heidi's eyes got even wider. "Okay, that *is* surprising," she admitted. "I swear I've seen Matteo look at you like..."

"Like he wants more?" Hillary said glumly. "Yeah. Well, Matteo is an amazing dominant, but he kinda sucks at the 'staying platonic' thing. There have been a couple of, um... you know."

Heidi nodded. She stabbed a piece of lettuce with her fork and chewed it thoughtfully. "The platonic dominant-submissive thing always seemed like one of those concepts that works in theory, but isn't so good in practice. In order for D/s to really work, there has to be a certain level of trust and focus, and it's hard to achieve that without an emotional connection. Plus, you know," she said, leaning closer and whispering, "spankings are freakin' hot." Heidi wiggled her eyebrows.

Hillary laughed and shook her head. "You don't need to tell me!"

Heidi smiled. "So, then... why did you want things to be platonic?"

Hillary grimaced. "Well... I didn't. Not at all, really. This was his idea. I would've been fine with, you know, the *real thing*. In fact, I want it so badly I can't even *tell* you. But... I figured out a while ago that I don't just want a dominant, I want *Matteo*. And this is what he wants. Dom-with-benefits. So I figured I'd take what I could get. I mean, I'm supposed to submit, right?"

Hillary took another deep gulp of her drink, feeling the cold and the alcohol rush to her head, and welcoming it.

"Heck, no!" Heidi said, outraged. "Consistently ignoring your own needs isn't *submission*! It's a recipe for *disaster*. Trust me on this one. And what does Matteo say when you talk to him about it? What's his rationale?"

"Heidi, I haven't said anything to him about this!" Hillary said. "Can you even imagine how that conversation would go? 'Gee, Matteo, I wish you'd sleep with me!' No way! He'd run for the hills. I keep waiting for it."

Heidi deflated. "Hillary, that's ridiculous. You *have* to talk to him. D/s *only* works if you're totally honest about communicating your needs. Matteo knows that. And frankly, I'm more than a little upset at him. He should be checking in with you, seeing where your head is at. I can only imagine he's distracted with all the other stuff going on…"

Hillary swallowed, near tears. "I'm frustrated," she admitted, her voice barely a whisper. "Sexually and emotionally. One minute he's kissing me like I'm the most important thing in the world, and the next minute I can practically feel a wall between us. I'm getting emotional whiplash!"

"I can imagine," Heidi agreed. She leaned across the table and whispered, too. "And no sex? Whatsoever?"

"Nope," Hillary said. "At least, not with me." And wasn't *that* an awful thought? "He *has* been hanging out at The Club a lot, though."

"Well, that's only because of the plan to catch Marauder, obviously!" Heidi soothed her in a low voice. "I mean, Dom said Master Blake and the guys have been putting things in place for *days* to exterminate that jerk and his nasty little minions. But now that Blake's wife was able to hack the email from Marauder and they know he's planning something at The Club tomorrow night, it'll only be a matter of time before they have enough evidence to bring charges against him! By the time I walk down the aisle, they'll have enough to put Marauder in jail, and then Matteo will be able to focus on your relationship! At least Matteo had *better* focus on it!"

Hillary felt her jaw drop and she shook her head dumbly.

"*What* plan, Heidi? What are you talking about?"

Heidi's eyes widened as she realized that she'd spilled the beans again. "No! *Hillary!*" she wailed. "You said you *knew* about the club!"

"I knew about the stuff *Marauder* did, not some plan to stop him! Spill it!" Hillary demanded.

Heidi shook her head vehemently. "No! Nope. I'm going to shut my mouth, *finally*."

"Heidi, you've *got* to tell me! Matteo won't!"

"No, I don't, sweetie," Heidi said, not without sympathy. "In fact, I think *not* telling you is the best thing I can do for you. You've got to find a way to talk to Matteo about this stuff. You've got to be able to *trust* him. You've been trying to deal with all of this stuff on your own—processing your fears about Marauder, and about your relationship. That's the *opposite* of what you need to do. You're blaming Matt for not knowing what he wants from your relationship. But, Hillie, you need to decide what *you* want."

Heidi's cell phone rang, and Hillary saw Dom's name on the display. "Gotta take this," Heidi said with a wink as she answered. Hillary nodded and heard her sister's soft "Hey, honey," as she stood up and walked toward the lobby.

Hillary toyed with her salad, pondering what Heidi had said. *Was* she doing the same thing she'd been blaming Matteo for? Had she been guilty of keeping her distance?

Nicole appeared at her elbow and set a small glass down in front of her, smiling like a Cheshire cat. The drink was a bright reddish-orange color, and didn't look like anything Hillary had ever had before.

Hillary smiled and shook her head in confusion. "I didn't order this," she told Nicole.

"I know! A guy at the bar ordered it for you, asked me to bring it to you along with this note! He's *super cute*, Hillie!" she squealed, wide-eyed.

A guy at the bar?

Hillary turned around and scanned the bar area, which was almost deserted at this hour of the day.

There was a portly guy with balding hair, and two older women. Definitely no cute guys.

"Where is he?" Hillary asked.

Nicole turned. "Over... *huh*. He's gone. That's weird," she said with a shrug. Then, regaining her enthusiasm, she handed Hillary a folded-up cocktail napkin. "Maybe he wants to remain mysterious!"

She gave Hillary a wink and left.

Hillary's neck prickled with foreboding as she scanned every table in the restaurant. No one who looked like Marauder. But suddenly she felt exposed and vulnerable.

She unfolded the note and scanned the contents.

Oh, God.

Hope you like this drink, bitch. It's called a Redheaded Slut. I thought it was appropriate, though I've gotta say, I like you as a blonde.

Your sister's almost as sexy as you are. When I finally get to fuck you, I'm gonna let her watch.—M.

Sweet Jesus.

Marauder had been here. *Here* in Tony's restaurant.

She needed to find Heidi and get out of here, get somewhere safe. But *where* was she safe when Marauder knew where she lived and he knew where she worked?

With shaking hands, Hillary took her cell phone from her purse and punched in a number. She stood up from the table on shaking legs and grabbed her purse, her heart racing, and made her way toward Heidi.

Matteo answered on the first ring.

"Honey," she whispered. "I need you."

Whatever doubts she had about what was between them, Matteo would keep her safe. That was one thing she would *never* doubt.

Chapter 8

It had been Hillary's voice on the phone. It hadn't been someone from the hospital, or Heidi, or someone else calling and telling him she'd been in an accident.

It was *Hillary's* voice on the phone. And if her voice was the one on the phone, then she had to be okay.

At least that's what he told himself, over and over, as he sped toward *Cara*.

Maybe her mom had been hurt, or... or she'd gotten a book contract, or something exciting like that. Or maybe she'd made a mistake and bounced a check and needed some help... God, something *normal* that everyday people struggled with.

Then why had her voice been hushed and shaky?

God*dammit*, he never should've let her go out alone without protection.

Hillary was strong and capable, and wouldn't have called him unless something was wrong. The adrenaline surged through him as he took the final turn into the parking lot of *Cara*, and screeched to a halt, slamming the door and shoving his keys in his pocket. He stalked through the front door—it would be quicker than navigating through the teeming kitchen—and quickly scanned the crowd. There she was, sitting with Heidi in the corner. Heidi was on the phone, and Hillary's eyes were wide and panicked as she gripped Heidi's hand, and even from where he was, he could see the utter terror on Hillary's face.

He could kill the bastard who put that look in those beautiful eyes of hers.

She got to her feet when he walked through the door, and her eyes said everything—the immediate relief upon seeing him, her little hands instinctively pulling away from Heidi and reaching for him. He got to her in three long strides and the hell with Heidi and Tony and the whole fucking establishment of *Cara* seeing him, he pulled her into his arms and kissed her forehead fiercely. She wrapped her arms around him, and a small gasp escaped.

"God, I'm glad you're here," she said, handing him a note with shaking hands. "He was here, Matt. Right here. He bought me this drink and gave me this note."

One arm holding her tightly against his chest, with his free hand he opened the note and read it.

"Son of a fucking bitch," he growled. He was tempted to crumple the paper in his hands and throw it but they'd need that fucking paper.

He had the sudden realization that he'd only *thought* he was angry before. Now, he felt fury so powerful it was a raging animal, pounding its hoofs with the hammering of his heart, rearing its head as it charged full force, ready to destroy, ravage, and plunder.

"He was here," she repeated.

Was?

Was the bastard still hiding, watching her terror unfold with glee, as her rescuer came riding in to save her? Did he get off on playing cat and mouse?

"Sit," he ordered, and though her eyes flickered at her momentary temptation to balk—he knew she wanted to remain gripped firmly in his arms—she'd been trained well enough to obey. She sat, but he still gripped her hand tightly as he looked to Heidi.

"Dom?" he asked as she hung up her phone.

"He's on his way," Heidi said.

Matteo nodded as he looked to Hillary. "How'd you get the note, baby?"

"Nicole gave it to me," Hillary whispered.

Matteo scanned the restaurant until he saw Nicole a few tables away, scribbling down an order. As he went to let go of Hillary's hand, she held on tighter and her eyes widened.

"Don't let go," she whispered.

"Baby, I just need to go get—"

"I'll get Nicole," Heidi interrupted, with a quick glance at the way Hillary's hand gripped his before she fled.

"Let's go to the break room," Matteo said. "This bastard's gotta be long gone." He led Hillary to the back room as Heidi followed with Nicole. Matteo gestured for Hillary to sit down as Nicole and Heidi came in the room.

"Hi, Matt," Nicole said, as she approached the table. He nodded and held up the napkin.

"Who gave this to you? I want every fucking detail," he said.

Nicole's eyes widened.

"What's the matter?" she whispered. He handed it to her to read. As she did, she lifted a trembling hand to her mouth.

"Oh my God," she said. "Hillary, I am *so* sorry. I had no idea that—"

"Who *gave* it to her?" Matteo repeated. "Think, Nicole. It's important." He turned quickly to Heidi. "Get Tony," he ordered before he turned back to Nicole.

"I—now that you ask, I really don't know," she whispered. "He was... tall, wearing jeans and a black sweater, glasses... oh! He had a scar on his right hand and a tattoo on his wrist."

Hillary's eyes closed. "That's him," she whispered. "Knife cut scar and a scorpion tat. He was here. Right here. Didn't even send his henchmen this time. He doesn't wear glasses, but they were probably just a prop."

Matteo's hands massaged her shoulders.

"This time?" Nicole whispered, as Tony and Dom burst through the doors of the break room.

Matteo filled them in as quickly as he could, and if he thought he'd been angry, he was pleased to see his fury matched when Tony and Dom read the note. All of them together would make a much better team of skull-crackers than him alone, though he felt he could rip the fucker's limbs with his bare hands.

"Fucking little *shit,*" Dom swore vehemently. "I'll fucking *kill* him."

"Easy, Dom," Matteo said. He had to be careful to let his own reaction not give him away, and if there was one thing he'd learned in his years in both the Marines and as a dominant, it was how essential it was to stay calm in the face of danger and emotionally-charged situations.

"We can't kill him until we fucking *find* him."

"You call the police?" Tony asked and Matteo shook his head.

"No," Matteo said with conviction. "I'll explain in a minute. First, Tony, you go lock the doors discreetly and no one goes in or out until Dom and I scour the place and lot to make sure he's gone." Tony ran to do what Matteo said.

He pointed to Nicole and Heidi. "You two stand on either side of her until Tony gets here. Got it?"

They nodded and assumed standing positions on either side of Hillary, who scowled.

"I don't need them to stand next to me," she protested. "I—"

Matteo interrupted her with a severe thrust of the finger in her direction. "Stay. Right. There." he ordered. She shrank, and nodded her head as he met Dom in the restaurant.

But as he suspected, there was no sign of Marauder anywhere. Fucking sneaky bastard.

They regrouped in the back room. "We don't call the police now. They get this type of shit every day and it's not gonna get us anywhere. Blake has a connection on the local squad that will get us a lot further as we dig up shit and I'll fill him in. So the next plan, we activate Blake and Slay." He turned to Dom.

Dom nodded. "Hell yeah." He faced Heidi. "And you. No way you're going home alone tonight." Heidi nodded obediently.

Matteo's jaw clenched as he faced Dom's eyes. It had to be said.

"Hillary stays with *me*."

Heidi stood between Dom and Matteo, her eyes going straight to Matteo.

"Please, Matt," she said, pleading. "Keep her safe."

For a fraction of a second he wondered again if Heidi knew more than she let on, but he had no time to dwell. He merely reached a hand out to Heidi and squeezed her hand, a brotherly gesture that said what needed to be said as Dom's eyes caught every detail.

Dom nodded. "Yeah. Hill stays with you."

Matteo met his eyes. "No one's touching a hair on her head."

"What was that all about?" Hillary asked, as they sped toward The Club.

"What?" he asked, his mind swirling with a plan of action and what had to be done.

"The standoff with you and Dom," she said. "You two staring at each other like—"

"Not now, Hillary," he said, more curtly than he intended to, and it wasn't lost on him how she pulled away a bit from the grasp he had on her hand. He sighed. The afternoon had been difficult for her, and she didn't need him being a pain in the ass.

But now wasn't the time to get into things with her about Dom, either.

"I'm sorry, baby," he said softly. "I don't want to talk about it now."

She nodded, as he gave her a sideways glance. He didn't want to give her shit, but he needed her on the same page.

"The better question is, why'd you give me shit about staying with Heidi and Nicole? Do you have any idea how important it is for you to obey me right now?"

Hillary shrank a bit as she nodded. "It was nerves," she said, waving her hand. "You know, nothing to be held into account by the whole—you *spank* me when I disobey thing—because, *if* you'll recall correctly, I didn't *exactly* disobey you, did I?"

He could help but smirk. Trying to get out of a spanking.

"That remains to be seen," he muttered.

"Matt!"

He sobered. "I will say this one more time, Hillary. Now is the most important time for you to obey me. You got me?"

She swallowed and nodded. "Yes, sir."

"Good girl," he praised. "Shit could go down, Hill, and I need to know you're listening. If I tell you to leave, or get to the car, or lock your door, or hit the floor, you fucking *obey*. You get me?"

"I do," she insisted. There was a brief pause as she cleared her throat.

"Is now the time you're going to tell me about the sting you have underway with Master Blake? Or are you going to keep me in the dark?"

He swore under his breath.

"Heidi?"

"If I tell you it was her, are you going to get her spanked?"

"You tell me everything or I pull this car over and *you're* the one getting spanked," he promised, and she knew he meant it as she began talking rapidly.

"Heidi thought I knew," she began, "so she didn't mean to tell me anything I wasn't supposed to know. She assumed you were telling me everything so... yeah, she told me there was a sting. And that I got flowers sent to me, which, ha, funny I don't remember anything about *flowers*, Matteo."

"Watch your tone," he warned. She was gonna need a good spanking when the night was over. High strung and stressed, he well knew a good, sobering session over his knee would help alleviate her stress and she would sleep better. But if she didn't watch out, stress or no, she'd end up over his knee for an entirely different reason.

"Matteo," she said with a sigh. "I'm sorry. I will speak politely. Promise. But please, I'm begging you. I would like to know about what's going on that involves *me.*"

His hand continued to hold hers, massaging in soothing circles as he thought. He hadn't wanted her to be afraid. He wanted her to feel *safe*.

"Matteo," she said, her voice a low, pleading whisper. "I can handle this. I'm not a child, or incapable of dealing with stressful situations."

"Fucking know you're not a child," he muttered, and the tension eased a bit as she giggled, and he contemplated telling her. It was too late anyway, if Heidi had told all.

"I know you're strong, and that you can handle it, Hill," he said, his hand still massaging hers. "That's not why I've held anything back. No, baby, not at all." He sighed. It was time.

"We suspect Marauder has people in The Club who work for him," he said. "Slay intercepted an invitation last week sent supposedly by Manny, only it wasn't Manny after all. Blake believes all his long-term employees and members are trustworthy—Manny, me, Slay, and a few others. But there are a handful of new hires that signed on since the shit went down at Black Box, one who even worked at Black Box, a domme named Rena. She and Slay go way back and he trusts her. Blake isn't so sure. What's tricky is that we're not sure it's someone who *works* for The Club, but could be a guest. And you know there are so many members and guests, it's taking freaking *forever* to narrow things down."

"Wow," she breathed. "Matteo... is there anyone else who's a target? Or is it just me?"

He paused. "We don't know. So far, it looks like you're the target for the *short* term, but it looks like the bigger picture here is Marauder is trying to bring down The Club." He shook his head. "Theory is, he gets you, word gets out that The Club was responsible for... whatever... the Club goes down. But, honestly, baby... Slay, Dom, and me, we're all convinced this is personal."

She sighed. "So you've got info," she said.

"Lots," he said. "And we'll show you in the back room, *if* Blake lets you in. So far the only people at The Club who know anything are me, Dom, Slay and Blake. Even Heidi doesn't know some shit."

They pulled into the parking lot as Hillary squeezed his hand.

"Thanks for telling me," she said.

He nodded. "Now be a good girl and do what I say," he ordered. She merely nodded, and he could tell she'd sobered.

Slay and Blake met them at the back door, the private entrance only Club staff had access to. Blake gave a courteous nod to Hillary, his eyes meeting hers in a protective, paternal glance.

"You okay, honey?" he asked in his deep, raspy voice.

She merely nodded, as Slay flanked her other side, both feet planted firmly on the ground, his arms crossed over his mammoth chest.

"We'll find the bastard," he promised. Hillary's eyes softened as she looked to both Blake and Slay.

"Thank you," she whispered, grasping Matteo's hand even tighter.

Giving a chin lift to Matteo, Slay led them through the door.

Matteo had a protective arm around Hill as they stepped into the back room. It wasn't enough to keep his gaze fixed on her. He needed his *hand* on her, cupping her elbow, holding her hand, grasping her wrist. It had been a mistake allowing her to go out alone. He'd allowed his judgment to get clouded in the heat of the moment earlier. It was a mistake he wouldn't make again.

Blake led them to a small back room Hillary had never seen before, but Matteo had visited a few times. A stranger stood by, a well-dressed man with graying brown hair, and a trim beard, wearing khakis and a button-down shirt.

"Inspector Mantle," Matteo said. "This is Hillary." They shook hands.

Mantle would, of course, already know who Hillary was, thanks to his investigation, but Matteo figured it would be best not to freak her out any further by explaining that.

The Club camera feeds, similar to those in Blake's office but larger, lined the walls, and there were yellow post-it notes attached to the walls with notes jotted down in thick black marker.

Blake gestured for Hillary to sit next to Matteo, as he pulled up his laptop and Mantle walked behind him, hands clasped behind his back.

"Hillary, I thank you for your cooperation in all of this," he began. "We've…" his eyes went to Matteo's for a moment, and he paused. "Surmised up to this point it was best you not be dragged into the details of this investigation, but it seems the time has come that you take part as we close in on being able to apprehend our suspects."

Hillary quirked an eyebrow at Matteo. She was no fool, and well knew that the reason they'd 'surmised it was best not to drag her in' had Matteo written all over it. Matteo met Hillary's eyes and merely nodded. He was not going to apologize or take it back. The past few nights she'd slept like a baby next to him, and ignorance, as far as he was concerned, was fucking bliss.

"I've pieced together past stories, and cross-referenced them to similar BDSM club scandals, stalking incidences, and assault charges we've had in the past few years. We were able to track Marauder's identity to New York City where he was removed from a BDSM club in Queens for 'non-consensual domming'." Mantle shook his head. "It was merely violation of a club rule, not necessarily illegal. And there were other incidences in various locations as well, but not everyone has as stringent laws regarding stalking and assault as we do here in Boston," he explained. "With a little investigation, it's become clear that this particular gentleman enjoys luring young, unsuspecting girls to a club where he takes advantage of them, and eventually rapes and batters them." Matteo's hands fisted on the table but Hillary remained unmoved. "There were four separate incidences that were on record at the club in Queens, but no one could identify the dominant. But each had identical stories, and notes on each claimed the scar and tattoo that we've now identified as belonging to Marauder." He shook his head. "Marauder not being his real name, of course. He has several but we've narrowed down his real identity to that of Marshall Griffson." Hillary shook her head, clearly unfamiliar.

"There's a warrant out for his arrest," Mantle said, "and just this evening, I've uncovered some information that will bode well in our favor when we apprehend him."

Matteo, Blake, and Slay sat straighter as Mantle opened a second folder.

"It seems our perpetrator has a taste for minors. In the past few months, there have been reports of a man meeting his description targeting minors, but again, no apprehension." He cleared his throat and his voice dropped. "There were two incidences of violation against a minor and the perpetrator is still at large."

At that, Hillary cringed, Slay swore, and Matteo felt the hot beast of fury clawing again at his chest.

Fucking *minors*. God, he hoped Dom or Slay would let him at the son of a bitch before they hauled him away.

Hillary swallowed. "So where do we go from here?"

Mantle closed the folder and took a deep breath, his eyes flickering to Matteo before he continued.

"That's a good question, Hillary," he said gently. "And my personal opinion is that the sooner we move, the better. If Griffson catches wind of our investigation, this entire operation could be at risk. We need to draw him out and apprehend him before he does any real damage. And certainly before he hurts anyone else."

Matteo eyed him warily. "What are you thinking?" he asked.

Mantle's lips pursed as he nodded thoughtfully. "Bait, Matteo. We need bait."

Matteo's gripped Hillary's hand so tightly she winced.

"Tell me more," he growled, and Blake stood.

"We're not putting her in harm's way," Matteo said. "Absolutely not. There has to be another way. She's been in his clutches once, and I'll be damned if she comes within ten feet of him on my watch."

Hillary cleared her throat, and they all looked to her.

She spoke softly, her eyes wide and earnest as she looked from Slay, to Blake, to Matteo.

"I can't even tell you how much I appreciate how protective you all are. Honestly, I am so grateful that you would go to such lengths to ensure my safety."

Matteo knew where she was going with this and he groaned inwardly as she continued. Damn it if she wasn't right, but God, he hated the idea of putting her at risk.

"But I agree with Inspector Mantle. If we are going to draw him out and end this, we need it done *now*. We don't have time to play games, and wait until he makes his next move. We do need bait, and it only makes logical sense that the bait is *me*." She paused as they all watched her quietly. "I'm not alone in this. We will plan my moves strategically, and I'll follow my instructions. But harm won't come to me." She paused. "I trust Matteo with my life."

Aw *hell*, why did she have to go and do that?

He squeezed her hand. Brave, beautiful, tenacious girl.

Matteo spoke up. "She's right. Hill's gotta be the one at the center of this operation so we can bring him down." He looked to Slay and Blake. "We protect her every fucking move. We get her just close enough to get him, and he doesn't touch a hair on her head."

Her eyes met his and they warmed, thanking him, as he reached for her hand and squeezed it, but he fixed her with his sternest, most sobering look and she nodded.

No screwing around.

He addressed the rest of them.

"Let's do this."

They drove in silence, heading back to his place, and his eyes were trained on the rear view mirrors. Though Mantle told them Griffson had a pattern that included a deliberate plant and withdrawal for a few days, Matteo didn't trust for a minute that they weren't being watched. Still, on the entire way home he noted nothing out of the ordinary.

Maybe it was part of the asshole's plan. Scare her shitless, then go lie in hiding for a while until she got comfortable again.

God, he hoped he'd be the one to get his hands on him first. Could he trust himself not to fucking *kill* him? Hillary's voice interrupted his thoughts.

"So, uh. I'm feeling a little hungry," she said. "I think all this drama has ramped up my appetite. I could totally go for some fries, or a burger. You?"

"I'm taking you straight to my place, and throwing the deadbolt on that fucking door. You're not going anywhere. We'll order takeout."

She sighed and reached for his hand, and it surprised him how the touch of her smaller, fragile hand in his calmed his fury.

"Matt," she said calmly. "If they're going to use me as bait, you need to be willing to put me on the line."

Put her on the line? *God*.

He'd been in battle before. He'd gone through boot camp and training for the Marines that drove lesser men to their knees. He'd been in the dark, dank recesses of foreign countries with his buddies, seen one lose a leg when a piece of shrapnel hit him not two inches from his knee, the screams and torrent of blood still vivid recollections that came to him in the middle of the night when he'd wake in a cold sweat. But never in his life had he felt such fear. The thought of her even *near* Marauder, much less touched or hurt by him…

"I trust you, Matteo," she whispered. "You won't let him hurt me. Why do you think I called you today before I did anything else?"

He swallowed. "God, Hill, if he touched you…"

"It would kill you. I know," she said, her voice catching. She looked troubled. "Well, I know after tonight, anyway…"

"What do you mean, *after tonight?*" he asked, as he took a turn and headed back to his place. "You questioned that before?"

"That you cared about me? Hell, yeah, Matteo. You go for weeks at a time without even *kissing* me. How am I supposed to know you care about me?" Her voice grew stronger as she pulled her hands away from him and sat up straighter in the passenger seat. "But after tonight, at least I'm convinced you *do* care about me."

Cared about her?

Jesus.

He inhaled. "Not bedding you has *nothing* to do with me not caring about you," he said, his own voice growing stronger as the infuriating unfairness of the situation hit him in the gut. "It's *because* I care about you that I'm not sleeping with you."

"That makes no sense!" she said, her voice rising now, and she was getting dangerously close to getting herself hauled over his knee. "Who the hell *doesn't* sleep with someone they *care* about?"

"Me! I don't! In fact, I haven't cared about any piece of tail I *have* slept with for fucking years!"

"Well that was a dumbass thing to do!" she snapped.

He inhaled slowly, and she immediately apologized.

"I'm sorry, Matt," she said. "That was—I shouldn't have said—I'm sorry," she repeated, as if she suddenly remembered she was his submissive and not allowed to speak rudely to him.

"I'm not going to spank you for that, Hill," he said wearily. He knew she was pent up and angry, and he didn't blame her. But he also knew she needed consistency from him, so he amended what he said. "But if it happens again, I will. Right now, we're both hungry, tired, and stressed out. I get it." He pulled into his apartment complex and parked the car. "And this is what we're going to do."

Her eyes were cast down at her hands as they twisted in her lap.

"We're going upstairs, and we're ordering food. You're also going over my lap." Her eyes flew to his and widened, but he shook his head. "Not going to punish you, baby," he said. "But I think a good session over my lap will help you put this night behind you. Keep you in your place, help you focus on your number one goal—being my good girl. I'll order us some food and you'll go to bed early. Understood?"

Her eyes softened, and she visibly relaxed. "Yes, sir."

He reached one hand out to her cheek and gently stroked.

"So strong. Such a good girl. Now you'll do what I say and behave yourself, yeah?" He reached his finger and thumb to a cute little strand of hair that stood askew and tweaked it. She smiled. It was the first smile he's seen all night, and it warmed him.

"Yes, sir," she repeated.

It killed him not to take her upstairs and lay her down and claim her as his.

But he would do right by her if it killed him.

Chapter 9

"Okay, Hillary," Master Blake said in her ear. "Visual is working. If you can hear me, tap your finger twice."

Hillary let her gaze wander around the main bar area of the club, and obediently touched her fingertip to the bar once, and then again, trying to appear nonchalant, as though she were waiting for someone.

"Perfect," Master Blake encouraged. "Crowd's pretty dead for a Thursday so far, but I'm guessing that will change soon enough. Remember the plan, honey—when Slay comes in, be flirtatious. Then Matt will do the jealous-thing, you'll have your fight, and Matt will be seen leaving The Club, clearing the way for Griffson to make his move. You'll come to the back room here to wait safely until we've secured the smaller dance floor, then you'll go dancing and draw him out. You just hang in there!"

Hillary fought the urge to roll her eyes.

Yeah, she'd reviewed 'the plan' exhaustively with Matteo, Slay, Dom, Inspector Mantle, and Master Blake earlier today until she knew her role backwards and forwards. But 'hanging in there' was easier said than done when you were sitting *alone* at a BDSM club, dressed in the tiniest, skankiest dress known to man, while the guy who'd held you captive, hurt you, and threatened to sexually assault you might be hiding somewhere on the premises, hoping to abduct you and finish the job.

No. *You wanted this*, she reminded herself. *You are here because you want to be here, because you want to help take him down.*

She took a deep breath and reminded herself of the words Matteo had spoken in Master Blake's back room earlier that evening, as he'd fitted the tiny communications device in her ear.

"Remember, honey, Blake's got every public area and employee area of the club on his monitors. Your comm device contains a chip that will track your location and a mic that'll let us hear everything you say. Plus, Blake will be directing all of us from the back room. You won't be alone for a minute."

The knowledge *almost* made her feel better, but there was a heavy feeling of anxiety in her belly that she couldn't seem to dispel.

She sighed and resisted the urge to fidget with her too-short white dress, chosen partly because it was appropriately sexy and partly because it would show up well on camera.

Maybe her anxiety had more to do with what *hadn't* been said.

She'd done what Heidi had told her to do, right? She'd let herself be vulnerable and told Matteo *flat out* that she didn't understand how he felt about her. And what was the sum total explanation and reassurance she'd gotten from him?

It's because I care about you that I'm not sleeping with you!

The words might have been spoken in English, but they made exactly *no* sense. If you were in love with someone, why wouldn't you want to sleep with them?

But Matt hadn't seen fit to enlighten her further. He'd taken her back to his house, ordered her takeout, given her a thorough-but-not-punishing spanking designed to relieve her stress and leave her boneless and sated, and tucked her into bed.

The spanking hadn't worked as well as he'd hoped, though,

because what was stressing her out was *lying in bed next to her* with his heavy arm wrapped around her waist. So she'd lain awake most of the night, listening to the sound of his breathing and trying to retrace the path that had gotten her here, so she could figure out where it had all gone wrong.

"Okay, let's test the audio quality," Master Blake said, startling her out of her thoughts. "Order yourself a drink."

Hillary stifled a smirk. She was being *told* to order a drink? Somewhere in this club, Matteo was scowling.

Good! How's that frustration feel, buddy?

The snarky words in her head brought her up short for a minute. She was glad that Matteo couldn't hear her thoughts through the earpiece, or she'd be in trouble for sure.

Hillary lifted a hand and signaled to the pair of servers, one blonde and one brunette, standing behind the bar. The cute blonde bartender rushed over.

"Hi," Hillary began with a smile. "Could I please have a—"

"Sam Adams?" the bartender interrupted. "Yeah, I remember!"

Hillary frowned and looked at the woman's face more closely.

"Wait, *Alice*?" she asked, in shock. "I almost didn't recognize you!"

Gone were the baggy shirt and girl-next-door make-up Alice had sported on Hillary's first foray into The Club. In their place were the ultra-sexy, tight white t-shirt and black leather miniskirt that most of the waitresses wore, along with dramatic black makeup that highlighted Alice's dark blue eyes. It was a complete transformation.

Alice shrugged and grinned broadly. "Well, I'm finally allowed to work the bar in *here*, where people actually *tip*, instead of out *there* in no-man's-land," she said, waving a disparaging hand towards the main club entrance. "Figured it was time to start dressing like a grownup so people would take me seriously!"

Hillary nodded in agreement, even as Blake's voice sounded in her ear.

"Ah, shit. Hey, Slay, if you're hearing this, I meant to mention that to you earlier, man. I know you asked me to keep her outside as a favor, but Gabby needed time off for a family emergency and Deb is too new and too green. It's temporary, so just roll with it. Oh, ah… by the way, Hillary, your audio's good."

Huh. Slay had asked for Alice to be assigned to the outer bar? Hillary made a mental note to investigate that further.

Alice set a beer bottle down in front of Hillary

"So, uh… how's Slay?" Alice asked. Her tone was just a touch *too* casual, and Hillary could tell that she was extremely interested in the answer.

"I have no idea," Hillary said honestly. "I haven't really seen him since the first night I was here."

Alice nodded speculatively.

The brunette bartender wandered over, propped a hip against the bar, and looked at Hillary insolently. "Haven't you heard, Alice? *This* chick isn't into *Slay*. She's attempting the impossible. She's trying to get Master Matteo off the market."

Hillary felt her face flush as she toyed with the label on her beer bottle. "Where'd you hear that?"

The brunette folded her arms across her chest and smiled widely.

"I saw it with my own two eyes," the brunette replied, still addressing herself to Alice. "Couple weeks ago, Matteo had her pushed up against the wall in the back hall, talking about spanking her. Saw her with him *again* last night. And *now* I hear they're shacked up. Is it true?" she demanded.

Alice's jaw dropped. "Jeez, Deb! Stalker, much?"

Deb shrugged. "Well, pardon me for noticing *every damn thing* a hot piece of ass like Matteo does. In a sea full of hot guys," she said, waving a hand to indicate the club and all its patrons, "he is the hottest by far."

Hillary clicked her teeth together. *Do not slap her! Stay in character! Lay the groundwork!*

"Well, I mean, he *is* hot," Hillary agreed, in what she hoped was a casual voice. "But all the *rules* are a little much for me, you know? Slay seems a little more laid-back, *and* he's cute! Don't you think?"

Alice blushed. "Ah... well... I don't know. I mean, Slay's not exactly laid-back, is he? And he's too big to be *cute*. But he can be really sweet sometimes."

"Sweet? God, Alice, you're *adorable*," Deb snorted. "If you care about personality with a guy like Slay *or* Matteo, you're completely missing the point. The only things you need to worry about are the way his hands can hold a flogger and the size of his... *Oooh, lawdy*! Would ya look who just walked in?"

Hillary and Alice both swung their gazes to the front of the room to watch Slay enter, his height and broad shoulders filling the doorway as his sharp-eyed gaze travelled around the room. His eye caught on Alice, then shifted to Hillary and held. He strode over.

"Well, if it isn't Tinker Bell," Slay said, leaning one forearm against the bar. His voice was deliberately pitched deeper, sexier, and raspier than she'd ever heard it. "And aren't you looking *fine* this evening?"

Yeesh. Despite knowing that it was all part of the plan, part of the setup, that voice was so potent that Hillary felt a very real blush wash over her cheeks.

"You here alone?" Slay demanded, scowling at her like the protective dominant he was.

Hillary cleared her throat and played her part. "Maybe," she said coyly.

On the other side of the bar, the two servers watched this exchange avidly, and Hillary saw Alice frown.

"Not safe, baby," Slay said, leaning towards Hillary and shaking his head in mock disapproval.

Hillary glanced at Alice quickly, and saw that her frown had become a scowl. *Shit.* She'd really started to like Alice, and prayed that someday Alice would forgive her for what was about to happen next.

Hillary slid her hand over to where Slay's arm rested, and entwined her fingers with his.

"Well, maybe you could keep me company," she whispered softly. "Then I wouldn't be alone anymore."

"*A-hem!*" Alice cleared her throat loudly.

Slay frowned and turned his head toward the noise.

"Why, young Alice," he said, as though he hadn't noticed Alice the moment he walked in the room. "Surprised to see you here." His voice said that he wasn't pleased, either.

Alice blinked uncertainly, but tried to tough it out. "Well, I *work* here, *remember*? Are you going senile already, old man?"

Deb snickered.

Slay smiled too, but it was the sort of smile that made Hillary shiver. "What I *remember* is telling you that your sass was going to get you in trouble one of these days, little girl," he said. "So why don't you hurry along and get back to *work*, while I finish my private conversation, hmm?"

Slay turned back to Hillary and didn't see the look of hurt and confusion that flashed in Alice's eyes before she slowly turned and walked to the other end of the bar.

"Now, where were we?" Slay asked Hillary, swinging one leg over to straddle the stool next to hers. "I think I was just about to sit here and keep you from feeling... *lonely*." He bit his lip and leaned even closer, so that Hillary could feel his breath on her face. "How'm I doin'?"

"Slay, this wasn't the plan," Blake's voice said in her ear.

Uh... no shit! This was so *not* in the plan.

Hillary swallowed and gave a nervous chuckle. "Oh, I'm feeling much better now," she said, attempting to glare at Slay discreetly since Deb was still watching them closely.

His eyes were twinkling with suppressed laughter.

"Hmmm... Nope, you still seem lonely," he mused. He grabbed her behind the neck and pulled her face even closer.

"Let me take care of that for you," he said. And then he pressed his warm lips to hers.

"What the ever-loving *hell*?" Blake's voice in her ear mirrored Hillary's own thoughts.

As Slay broke the kiss, Hillary gasped in shock. A second later, her gasp was mirrored by Deb's excited one, and Hillary knew the shit was about to hit the fan.

Matteo had arrived.

Hillary barely had time to formulate the thought before Matteo had grabbed the back of Slay's shirt with his left hand and forcibly hauled him off his stool.

"What. The. Fuck?" Matteo gritted out.

"Oh, Matteo!" Hillary cried, jumping up to stand between them. "No! It's not what you think!"

"No? Because I think I just walked in to find *you* kissing this *asshole*, right here in my club!" he spat.

Hillary forced herself not to cower at the heat of his gaze, and she knew that part of his anger was very real—Slay had gone way off-script, and she had gone along with it.

"Easy, man!" Slay said, his voice shaking with laughter. "I was just keeping Tink company for a minute!"

"*You don't get to call her that!*" Matteo roared. Then he swung his right hand into Slay's jaw with a sickening *crunch*. The force of the punch knocked Slay's head back and had him stumbling over his bar stool, but he recovered quickly.

He surged to his feet with his eyes narrowed. "Enough, man. I'll give you that one, but now we're even."

"Fuck you!" Matteo spat. He reared back and delivered another blow, this one hitting Slay in the nose. "*Now* we're even."

He dropped Slay onto the stool to cradle his bleeding nose in his hands.

"*Matteo!*" Hillary screamed, pulling at his arm in earnest. "Seriously, calm down! He's your *friend!* This was not a big deal; it was just…"

"Not a big deal!" Matteo whirled on her. "Is that right?"

"He *startled* me!" Hillary defended. "I didn't want him to!"

"That's a lie!" Alice said unexpectedly, and all eyes turned toward her.

Alice shrank under the scrutiny, but managed to whisper at Hillary accusingly, "You were flirting with him." She turned to Slay, and said in a clearer voice, "And worse, *you* were letting her. And to think, you're worried about *my* attitude getting *me* getting in trouble." She shook her head at Slay in disgust. "Call Jackie to cover when you leave, Deb. I'm taking my break," she said, and she stalked out.

"Fuck," Hillary heard Slay mutter under his breath.

Hillary swallowed.

Shit.

"Get back on script, Hillary!" Blake warned her.

Right. Okay. *But what was the script again?*

"Matteo, you have no right to be jealous!" Hillary said loudly. "You've been seeing other girls!"

"That's right. He has!" Deb interjected, slapping her palm on the bar. "Double standards are bullshit!"

Matteo's fists clenched, and the words tumbled out before Hillary could stop them. "After all, you don't even really *want* me!" she cried.

The crowd around them whispered and tittered, but Hillary was focused on Matteo. His eyes had narrowed, as though he realized there was truth behind her hasty words.

"You are going to get the spanking of your life," Matteo said in a low voice, and she knew that his words weren't an act, either.

Crap.

Hillary forced herself to stand up straighter, and braced a

hand on her hip. "Um, *no*, I'm *not*," she told him. "I'm done with this. I'm done with *you*."

"What did you say?" Matteo asked, folding his hands over his chest and looking at her in a way that would have made her knees knock under any other circumstances.

"I said… I'm done," she said shrilly. "It's over between us!"

Matteo inhaled sharply.

"Fine," he bit off. "Then you can get your own fucking way home."

He stalked out of the room towards the employee area, and the crowd of people that had gathered parted in the face of his fury.

God.

"Don't stop now, Hillary," Master Blake whispered in her ear. "Finish it!"

Hillary swallowed and turned towards Slay.

"Hey, um, Slay, do you want to…" she offered, laying a hand on his shoulder.

Slay stood up, dislodging her hand.

"You know, Hillary, I suddenly remembered why I don't do relationships. Take care, honey," he said. And then he patted her awkwardly on the shoulder and walked away, in the opposite direction from the way Matteo had gone.

Hillary stood there for a moment, biting her lip. She knew her cheeks were flaming. *Wow*. The whole point was to make her seem defenseless, friendless, and ripe for whatever plot Marauder had in mind. She just hadn't expected the humiliation to feel quite so real.

"Jesus, he left!" someone whispered. "Matteo *actually* left her. I just saw him drive off!"

Furious whispers erupted.

"I can't believe he actually left!"

"Shit, have you ever seen him so pissed?"

"I would *die* if my dom ever looked at me that way!"

And finally…

"I guess the blonde is fair game now, huh?"

Hillary took a deep breath. Mission accomplished.

She turned and pretended to flee in the direction of the ladies' room.

A moment later, Inspector Mantle was holding open the door to Master Blake's back room for her.

"You did really well, honey," he said, guiding her to a chair behind Blake's desk.

"And Dom just called to say his Matteo impersonation is as slick as ever," Blake interjected from the other side of the room, as he slid his cell phone back into his pocket. "Matteo went into the basement, Dom took his keys, left out the back door, and got in Matt's car. He's on his way to get your sister from her friend's house."

"Great," Hillary said softly. "I heard a bunch of people talking about it before I even left the bar. That identical-twin thing comes in handy, I guess."

Blake nodded, then looked at her sympathetically. "Hell of a scene, huh?"

"Yeah," Hillary agreed. "Hit me harder than I expected. I think Slay and I are going to have words about his little improvisation back there!"

"Pretty sure Matt did the talking with his fists," Inspector Mantle told her. He rested his hip on the desk and shook his head admiringly. "Alex Slater is one crazy son of a bitch. I don't know whether I want to shake his hand or hit him again."

"Um, that's because *you* weren't the one getting kissed, sir," Hillary told him. "I *definitely* wanna hit him."

Blake chuckled and nodded. "True. If it had been my wife getting kissed, I would've laid him out flat. But shit, the way

Matteo decked him sold it. The crowd bought it, hook, line, and sinker. I almost believed it was real, and I knew better!"

Hillary smiled politely, but she didn't find it funny. As far as she was concerned, it had all been a little *too* real.

"All right, honey," Blake said, as Mantle stood up and brushed his hands on the legs of his pants. "We're gonna go and do *our* part now, and see if we can't nail that crazy mother—uh… that crazy *stalker* to the wall. Matt should be up here in a few minutes. In the meantime, you stay here and keep this door locked. You gonna be okay?"

Hillary gave them both a sincere smile this time. "Yeah, I'll be okay."

Mantle lifted his chin, Blake winked, and they both slid out the door, taking care to lock it behind them.

Hillary sat back in the chair, exhausted. She took the comm device out of her ear and tossed it on the desk.

She was so not cut out for the spy business.

Yeah, the whole thing had been staged, but it had hit a little too close to home. She needed to talk to Matteo and *demand* some answers.

She snorted, imagining how Matteo would react to that. Okay, scratch that. She'd state her needs in a respectful way.

She smiled to herself.

Movement on one of the video feeds caught her attention. Matteo and Slay, entering what looked like a storage room, where heavy-duty shelving held stacks of boxes and storage bins. Without thinking, Hillary reached out, snagged Master Blake's mouse and clicked on the feed, engaging the audio.

"What the fuck was that about, Slay?" Matteo demanded, leaning back against a shelf, his arms folded across his chest.

"Oh, come on, Matt," Slay said. He stood across from Matt, so that only his profile was visible, but from the congested sound of his voice, it was clear Matteo's fists had done a number on his nose. "I was just messing with you! I'll apologize to her, okay?"

Hillary nodded. *Darn right, he would.*

"Damn right you will," Matteo muttered. "But I wanna know what the hell made you do it in the first place! You were supposed to flirt with her, dickhead. You weren't supposed to get all up in her face, and you sure as fuck weren't supposed to kiss her!"

Slay snorted. "Well, *you* weren't supposed to set me up with a chick and end up taking her home yourself! Pretty shitty thing for a friend to do. So I figured I'd get my own back. Didn't expect you to lay into me! *Shit*. You being outraged on her behalf is cute and all, but since when do you care if someone gives a chick you've been banging a one-second, no-tongue kiss?"

Some chick you've been banging...

Hillary's blood ran cold.

"Shut the fuck up," Matteo growled. "It's not like that."

"I mean, *Christ*," Slay continued, as though Matt hadn't spoken. "A month ago, you were setting me up with this girl. 'Slay, I've got a girl who's like a sister, she needs a dom.' Then all of a sudden..."

"I. *Said*. Shut. The. Fuck. Up," Matteo said, taking a step away from the shelf, his voice flat and cold. "You don't fucking talk about Hillary that way."

"What do you mean I can't... *Oh*. Oh, *shit*, man!" Slay's voice held dawning wonder, and he stood straighter. "You're *gone* for her! You're in *love*! Jesus! Why didn't you say so, fucker? I never would've touched her if you'd told me she was *yours*!"

Hillary held her breath, then let it out with a shudder when she saw Matteo's face. He looked utterly horrified.

"That's not it, asshole! She's not *mine*. I mean, yeah, she's my *sub*, okay? But she's not... we're not... I haven't even had sex with her. I *can't*!"

"You... can't?" Slay repeated. "Bro, you talking about a physical problem?"

Under any other circumstances, Hillary would've giggled at the outrage on Matt's face.

"Fuck you! Hell, no! I can barely fucking control myself when she's around!" Matteo said.

Hillary felt a momentary burst of pleasure. *I knew it!* But that pleasure fled as soon as Matteo opened his mouth again.

"It's just... Hillary is young. She's sweet. She's got this misplaced gratitude thing going on because I helped her out at Black Box last spring. So, I promised Heidi I'd help keep an eye on Hillary, and... I'm not gonna take advantage, okay?"

Slay blew out a breath and ran a hand through his hair.

"Yeah, man, I get that. Better than you know."

Unfortunately, so did Hillary.

"But," Slay continued. "I still say..."

Hillary couldn't listen anymore. With a trembling hand, she reached out and clicked the 'minimize' icon.

So... *that* was what it meant when he said he wouldn't sleep with her *because* he cared about her. God, what an idiot she'd been. He cared about her, as a friend. He loved her, but like a sister. And yeah, he was attracted to her, but he was fighting it because, for Heidi's sake, he didn't want to treat her like all the... how had he put it last night? Like all the *pieces of tail* he'd slept with over the years.

Well. That's something, anyway.

Suddenly the room was too close, the air too hot. Her stomach clenched and rolled in humiliation, and tears burned behind her eyes. Blake had said Matt would be on his way upstairs to wait with her until they'd secured the dance floor for the next part of their plan, but she could *not* see him right now. She needed time alone to steel herself against the hurt, to put on a brave face... to figure out how to end things with Matteo, for once and for all.

She grabbed her purse from the corner where she and Matteo had thrown their stuff when they'd arrived a few hours ago. She wanted nothing more than to go home and crawl into bed, and to hell with the guys and their precious plan… But she couldn't. She remembered the way Slay had hurt Alice, the determination on Inspector Mantle's face… They'd all risked something to make this happen tonight, and she couldn't just duck out. She'd never be able to live with herself.

She took a deep breath and thought quickly.

Okay, so she'd make her way down to the dance floor now, before anyone could stop her. She'd stand there and have a drink, in full view of the cameras, and not talk to anyone. How dangerous could that be, really?

But first she had to get downstairs.

Steeling her spine, she eased the door to Blake's office open. The coast was clear. She walked carefully down the center of the carpeted hallway, pausing in front of each open doorway, until she was almost at the back staircase that led to the rear exit.

Almost there!

Voices from the stairway startled her. *Crap!* Matteo would be coming up those very stairs! Without thinking, she scuttled back down the hallway and ducked into one of the empty employee changing rooms, closing the door softly behind her.

God, but that had been close.

"Well, well, what have we here?"

The mocking voice behind her had her spinning around and falling back against the door with a squeak, but it was only Deb, the bartender. She was leaning over the Formica vanity in the back of the room, reapplying a coat of bright red lipstick, and she regarded Hillary's reflection with a raised eyebrow.

Hillary closed her eyes and let her heartbeat settle. "Sorry! You startled me!" Hillary said.

Deb smirked. "Uh… Last I checked this was the *employee* change room, and *you* don't work here, so…"

Hillary nodded. "Okay, right. Fair point. I guess I startled you first. I, uh…" Hillary glanced back at the closed door, and then at Deb. "I… was heading downstairs, but I have someone I don't want to run into out there."

Deb fluffed her brown hair. "Uh huh. Running from the masses because you pissed off two of the most popular dominants in the club tonight?"

"Uh… kinda, yeah," Hillary agreed. She was almost tempted to spill the whole sorry story to Deb, but she had to find a way out of here first.

Deb smiled. "Well, no judgment here, sister. In fact, I was looking for you a couple of minutes ago! Wanted to give you a high-five and buy you a drink!"

"Uh… you did?" Hillary asked, distractedly. "I thought you had a thing for Matteo."

Deb shrugged. "Meh. He's hot, but he's kind of a pussy from what I've heard. Nothing too rough, doesn't like to get his hands dirty. Hard to respect a guy with too many rules, you know?"

Hillary frowned, but before she could refute this, Deb spoke again.

"Besides, you know Matteo's not the kind of guy who'd ever be satisfied with just one woman, right? Some guys are just like that. Heck, my *own* dominant is like that. And it's fine if you're cool with it, but I'm sensing that you're *not*."

Hillary's heart sank and she bit her lip. "That would be… accurate."

Deb spun around.

"Figured. So, you need to escape? Just so happens, I know a way. A *secret* way," she said, fluttering her fingertips excitedly.

Hillary looked at her skeptically. "You do? I thought you'd only worked here a few months?"

Deb waved this away with a laugh. "Yeah, but I'm *motivated*. Blake has this stupid policy about employees staying out of the private rooms during shift, you know? 'We don't want to encourage fraternization with the members,'" she said, in pitch-perfect imitation of Blake's deep voice. She rolled her eyes. "So he sits there behind his millions of cameras and thinks he's got it all covered."

Something about this struck Hillary as odd, but Deb grabbed her arm and gave her a wink.

"He should never underestimate the willpower of a girl who wants to meet her dominant when she's supposed to be on break," Deb told her.

Hillary smiled.

Deb opened the door to a narrow closet on one side of the vanity, and Hillary stepped closer to peer inside.

"Um… Are we going to Narnia?" Hillary asked.

"Ha! Better!" Deb replied. "The attic." Deb moved aside a couple of garment bags to expose… a hidden staircase leading upstairs.

"Follow me," she said, and she led the way up the narrow stairs.

Hillary hesitated. Maybe the hallway was clear by now, and she could get down the stairs on her own…

Then she remembered the stupid cameras. If Matt or Blake or *anyone* saw her heading downstairs before the place was secured, they'd be after her in a heartbeat, full of worry and indignation, forcing her to explain herself.

And was pretty sure she would rather do *anything* than humiliate herself that way.

"Come on, Hillary," Deb called. "Are you coming?"

Hillary squared her shoulders, took a deep breath, and followed Deb up the dark stairs.

"See, in the olden days, this staircase led to the servants' rooms on the upper floor. There are a dozen rooms up here now that members can rent out when they need privacy, but there's also a staircase that leads directly to the basement! So, as long as Blake hasn't rented out the room to a member, we can… *yes!*"

Deb pushed the door at the top of the stairs open and

stepped out into the room. "No members up here!" she giggled, holding the door open for Hillary to squeeze past her.

The room was hot and dimly lit, the curtains closed so that only the faintest hint of streetlight shone through to illuminate the room. Hillary groped blindly along the wall to her right, trying to find a light switch, when a sudden noise from the bed in center of the room made her jump.

"Deb, I thought you said the room was empty!" Hillary whispered furiously, her heart pounding.

"No, Hillary. I said there were no *members* up here," Deb said, not troubling to keep her voice low. "My Master isn't a member of The Club 'cause he doesn't like to play by their stupid rules."

In the weak light, Hillary saw a figure stand up from the bed and turn on a lamp.

"Hillary knows all about the rules I follow. Don't you Hillary?" Marauder asked.

Hillary screamed, and the world went black.

Chapter 10

Matteo had so much adrenaline pumping through him he would've been disappointed if Marauder didn't show up for the party. Between Slay's fucking antics kissing Hillary, words with Slay, and the whole fake break-up scene which left him feeling like shit, he was ready to knock some heads together. But he didn't want Hillary to read his fury and frustration. He took a deep breath and calmed himself before he entered the room where she was supposed to be waiting for him. He pushed open the door, ready to be 'on' for her, to calm her and remind her how things would go down next. Ready to take down the asshole Marauder.

But she was not in the room. He looked wildly around for a minute and he almost knocked into Slay as he froze at the entrance of the room.

"Where the fuck is she?" Slay ground out. "She's supposed to be *here* first and then we're supposed to get a read on her on the dance floor."

No shit.

Her earpiece was on the table. Matteo knew it was hers as each was marked with a tiny color on the inside to identify them, and hers was pink. He'd even joked with her as he placed it in her ear earlier that evening, 'pink for Tink'. No one else had a pink mark.

And no one else had left their earpiece on the fucking *table* in the middle of the fucking *sting.* He looked quickly to where he and Hillary had put their belongings earlier and noticed her bag was gone. He breathed a bit easier. If she'd been abducted, likely her pursuer wouldn't have thought to take her bag.

So she'd left.

Matteo was *pissed* at her. He already told her she was getting the spanking of her life tonight and so help him, would she ever. She wouldn't sit for a week when he was done with her. How could she leave at a time like this?

He stepped into the room with Slay and shut the door.

"Her ear piece," he said to Slay. "And her bag is gone." He touched his ear and waited until he heard the responding clicks from Mantle and Blake.

"Where the hell is Hillary?" Matteo said. "Her ear piece is in the room, her bag gone, and she's not fucking here."

"Did she go to the dance floor already?" Blake asked, and Matteo spun to look at the cameras. "Third row center," Blake said.

But as Matteo's eyes went to the screen that showed the dance floor, it caught the image just to the right of the dance floor—the monitor showcasing the storage room where he and Slay had just been. Matteo groaned as he turned to Slay.

"The fucking *camera!* Damn it. She was *in here.* All she had to do was click on the audio and she'd have heard the whole fucking conversation we just had."

"Yeah? What does that have to do with anything?"

Matteo wanted to shake him, but instead he just shook his head as Blake's voice came back on his earpiece.

"You see her?"

He was scanning the camera feeds but he knew, with a

sinking sensation in the pit of his stomach, he would not see her. No sign of the little dress, her blonde hair, or her figure on the screen. Where the fuck *was* she? Snagging his phone out of his pocket, he jabbed at the screen and called her, but wasn't at all surprised when it went to her voice mail.

"No," he said. "I think she left."

"You think she *left!* What the *fuck!* Well, go after her. Damn it, Matteo!"

"No shit, but I don't know where she went!"

Footsteps pounded in the hallway and Slay and Matteo met each other's eyes for one quick second before the door to the room burst open and Alice came running in.

"Matteo! Slay!" she said, her eyes wide and panicked. Matteo felt cold fear creep along his limbs as he turned to face her. In her hand she held Hillary's phone.

"She was in the employees' changing room," Alice whispered. "I saw her go in, with Deb. And she dropped her phone. I didn't want to intrude so I gave them a few minutes and then followed behind them to give it to her. Knocked on the door and there was no answer, which was weird, so I went in, and... they were gone. Just like they *vanished*. It was... I don't even know. She's gone, Matteo."

It took all of thirty seconds to get Blake and Mantle in the back room, as Matteo paced and swore, scouring every camera feed, and Slay filled Alice in on what was going down.

"I don't know how to work these things!" Matteo growled. "We need to fucking rewind them! How do you rewind them?"

Alice told her story to Blake and Mantle, and before she was done Blake was already zoning in on the camera right outside the employees' room.

"It's illegal to have a camera in a private area," Blake

explained. "Expectation of privacy and all that. Could get sued. But maybe we can at least see how they got out."

He rewound it and they all watched as Deb entered the changing room, and shortly afterward Hillary opened the door to the changing room as well, her phone falling out of her bag. Then they saw Alice stoop and pick up the phone. Alice opened the door and a moment later came out with a puzzled expression on her face.

"I'm telling you, they vanished," she said. Matteo jumped as the phone in his pocket rang.

He didn't recognize the number. Dread crept over him, and he knew he had to answer.

"Hello?"

"Why, hello Master Matteo," came a low, calculated voice on the other end.

"Who is this?" Matteo demanded, and all eyes in the room went to him.

"Oh, you know who this is," came the low drawl. "We had a chance meeting at Black Box last year, didn't we?"

Matteo fisted his hand so hard it hurt. "Where is she?" he hissed.

"Far away from you," came the voice. "Maybe you shouldn't have left her alone. But you see, I'm not a cruel man. I thought you'd like to hear her while she joins me in a little *threesome.*"

"You son of a—"

"Matteo!" came Hillary's scream on the other end of the line. "The closet!" There was a loud thump and a wail and the phone went dead.

"Son of a bitch!" Matteo swore. "He's fucking got her. She yelled closet. What the *fucking* hell?"

"How much do you know about Deb?" Mantle was asking Blake, but Matteo was already out the door with Slay and Alice on his heels.

"Matteo!" Blake shouted.

"Checking the damn employee room," he responded and he was on his way.

They reached the employees' room and Matteo yanked the door open, but it was vacant. It was a small room, a break room of sorts with a dorm-sized refrigerator, table, and several small stalls for employees to change for a scene or to serve. He kicked open each stall and even hoisted himself up to where a small curtain covered a tiny window, but the only window in the room was far too small for anyone to fit through.

"What the *hell*," he murmured, staring at the walls and shaking his head. There had to be a way they escaped, or else they were still in the room. He tore through the cabinets again, but they were empty.

"She said the closet," Matteo muttered, and he yanked open the closet next to the vanity, though it made no sense.

"Is there a vent in here?" Alice asked, peeking her head in. "Or some kind of a window? If we just—ooohh!" She gasped as she moved the garment bags aside and pointed a trembling finger at a narrow, hidden staircase.

Matteo swore, pushed past her, and they all instinctively moved as quickly and as soundlessly as possible.

"Private rooms," Matteo whispered, as soon as they came to the top of the stairs. "These are the private rooms Blake rents out. You access them from the main club with a key and passcode, but he hasn't let them since we started the operation." Matteo leaned into Alice.

"Go down to Blake and Mantle," he handed her his earpiece and showed her how to use it. "You tell them what we found, and tell Blake I said I want security at the entrance of the private rooms." She nodded. "Go!" he hissed, as he and Slay moved wordlessly down the hallway. They could hear the faintest sound of voices in the room ahead.

"You little bitch," said a female voice. "Think you can get him to come and rescue you now?" Her voice trailed off and Matteo had to listen hard. Hillary's voice was stronger.

"You don't know Matteo," she said. "He'll find me." Her voice ended in a strangled gasp, and Matteo felt fury pumping through every inch of his body.

A deep, cruel male chuckle responded and there was a sickening sound of metal clicking into place and a low scream. God, what were they doing to her? He'd kill them. He'd fucking *kill* them. He and Slay crept along, and he was thankful he'd worked with Slay before, thankful they both had military training, the two of them wordlessly communicating in the face of danger and rescue, not knowing exactly what lay ahead of them.

"We're gonna record every minute of this and send it to your fucking *dominant*," came the voice.

Matteo stood on one side of the door and Slay the other. Slay gestured to the doorknob and then lifted his shoulder, a demonstration of what he was about to do. Matteo nodded. Slay would try the door knob, prepared to knock the door down, giving Matteo room to charge, and hopefully taking Hillary's captors by surprise.

Matteo didn't fucking care if there were ten of them. He'd fucking kill them all before they realized he'd even come in the room.

It was a solid door, meant to give the occupants privacy, but if anyone who knew how to take a door down it was Slay. It'd been his specialty when they were deployed.

Matteo held up three fingers. "On three," he mouthed.

Three.

Two.

One.

Slay tried the knob, found it locked, and with a swift move, ran back and heaved himself at the door. He broke through it with a loud grunt, and Matteo was right behind him. The scene that met his eyes had him seeing red before he charged—Hillary tied by all fours to the bed, stripped, Deb a few feet away holding a phone, frozen in the midst of recording, and Marauder, a fistful of Hillary's hair in his hands, stripped to the waist. Matteo caught him with a right hook before Marauder had a chance to respond, and Slay had his massive arms wrapped around Deb who screamed and tried to get away but was helpless to move.

Matteo knew he could kill Marauder with his bare hands, right now, and never look back. He landed another vicious punch to Marauder's stomach, which left him doubling over, gasping, and before he could recover, Matteo hit his jaw. Marauder gave a scream of rage and lunged back at Matteo, but Matteo was too quick. He dodged the attack, and punched Marauder so hard he felt and heard a satisfying crunch and knew he'd broken ribs. As Marauder reeled from the blow, Matteo heaved him up and shoved him against the wall, one solid punch after another landing in rapid succession. He was dimly aware of the screams from Deb, and that others had entered the room from another entrance—Mantle, Blake, and Alice—but he could concentrate on nothing but putting a decided end to the terror and assault Marauder had inflicted.

Blow after blow fell and still, his rage blinded him.

Someone pulled him off, and he heard Slay's voice in his ear. "I'd be happy to see you kill him, man, but you don't want to go there today. You're gonna hate me now but thank me later."

And hard as Matteo tried to get away, writhing, wanting to finish the beating, he couldn't. Slay was too strong, holding him in a vise-like grip.

Matteo slowly came to his senses, realizing that Marauder lay bloody and unconscious on the floor, Deb was cuffed on her knees with Mantle over her, and Alice was undoing the restraints around Hillary's wrists.

Hillary.

Oh, God, she'd seen his vicious loss of self-control. He felt sick as he watched Alice cover her in a blanket. He had no recollection of going to her, but the next thing he knew Hillary was cradled in his arms, sniffling into his shoulder, one little hand flat against his chest, the other still protectively tucked up against her.

"I knew you'd come," she whispered. "I didn't know how but I knew you would."

He wanted to carry her straight home, back to his place, where he could wash away the ugliness of the evening, hold her close, and bring her peace. He knew it wasn't time yet for that, and that he'd be patient. But there was one thing he knew for sure.

He was never going to let her go.

The debriefing took place in the back room with Blake, Mantle, and the rest of the crew. Marauder and Deb were taken away in handcuffs, with a laundry list of accusations and felonies that were bound to lock both of them away. Deb had confessed to being the one that had drugged the employees of The Club, slipping 'vitamins' to unsuspecting victims, and passing information on to Marauder. A subdued, brave Hillary met the questions of everyone there. When she was being questioned about whether or not Marauder had raped her, Matteo had held his breath.

"He tried," she said, as Matteo's hands clenched into fists and he focused on deep breathing through his nose while counting to ten in Italian, "but I kicked him so hard in the nuts he hit me instead, and then tied me up. But that was when Matteo came and saved me."

Kicked him in the nuts.

That's my girl, he thought. *Takes shit from no one.*

"She needs to go home now," he'd said, after calling Dom

and Heidi and filling them in with every single detail. Dom was on the other end of the line, swearing and fuming. He'd done the job of driving away and giving Marauder the illusion that Matteo was gone, but had been told to stay away from The Club by Mantle. It was too risky. According to Heidi, he'd been pacing their living room ever since, and the two of them were relieved to get the call.

"You can bring her here tonight," Dom said. "We have a spare room."

Matteo took the phone into the hallway and shut the door so Hillary would not hear.

"Are you *fucking* kidding me?" he said.

Silence on the other end of the phone. And then, "I'm just saying she may not want to be alone after all that, and she might want to be with her sister," Dom insisted.

Matteo rubbed a weary hand over his eyes and inhaled, calming himself. "She wants to be with me, Dom, and she will be."

Another pause, before Dom spoke again. "For tonight," he said.

"We'll talk about this later," Matteo said, hanging up the phone and shutting it off.

He did not care anymore what Dom thought, or what Dom said. Dom had been insistent that he not get into bed with Hillary, because Dom knew Matteo hadn't been dependable or committed when it came to women.

That was then.

This was now.

Matteo went back into the room and linked a hand around Hillary's.

"Taking her home," he said, nabbing her bag and his coat from the corner of the room. Blake nodded.

"Day off tomorrow, Matt," he said, and Matteo nodded his thanks. Matteo watched as Alice threw her arms around Hillary impulsively, and Hillary hugged her back. He reached out as they pulled away and squeezed Alice's hand.

"Thank you," he said with meaning, and she nodded shyly. Slay stood watching all of them, arms across his massive chest, still looking as furious as ever at the shit that'd gone down.

"You did good, girl," he said to Alice in a husky voice and Alice's face flushed pink. She looked at the floor and bit her lip, but nodded meekly.

Slay reached for Hillary and gave her a chaste, brotherly hug under Matteo's watchful eye.

"Stay close to him, babe," Slay said low. "He's got you."

Hillary pulled away as Matteo took her hand.

"I know," she whispered, as he led her away from the others and with decided steps, not looking back, out of the doors of The Club.

He'd be happy if she never set foot in there again.

And after tonight… shit was going to change.

Hillary hadn't said much of anything on the ride home, and he let her remain quiet. He was not going to probe, or push, or make her talk. If she wanted to talk until three in the morning, or wake him up in the middle of the night to tell him about what had happened, or if she never wanted to talk about the fucking night again, he'd be fine with it. Whatever she wanted, he would allow it. This was about her now. He'd done enough fucking this whole thing up.

And now it was time to make things better.

So it surprised him when they got to his apartment—she didn't even question that's where they were going—and he brought her upstairs, that she spun around and put both hands on her hips. Her eyes flashed at him as she looked at him and he waited tersely. What the hell?

"I shouldn't have left," she said, and she swallowed hard. He suddenly realized she was trying to be brave, to say whatever it was she needed to say. "I saw you on the monitor with Slay, and I heard the whole thing. You saved me, Matteo. But you need to know that we're through."

He nodded thoughtfully. How he would proceed now would be crucial.

"You heard what between me and Slay?" he asked. "And did it occur to you that you got spanked once for eavesdropping and I might not take too kindly to you doing it a second time?"

She'd been trained well enough that panic flashed through her pretty eyes before she nodded and lifted her chin bravely.

"That might be true if I were your submissive," she murmured. "And... you know I will forever be grateful for you saving me tonight. But I'm not going to allow you to discipline me anymore. Because I'm not... obedient to you."

He leaned back against the couch and nodded.

"And why is that?" he asked, even though it was taking all his willpower to stay calm and not get pissed off at what was going down.

Her eyes grew sad, and he marveled at her ability to have this conversation after the ordeal she'd just been through. "Because you don't love me," she whispered. "Not the way I need to be loved. You love me like a sister. Like a friend. And it doesn't work, me submitting myself to you, opening myself up like that." She drew a shaky breath. "I cannot—no, *will* not submit to someone who doesn't want me as his *lover*. It's too painful. Too hard. And I won't do it. Yes, I've fallen in love with you. You *know* that. And I—"

He'd heard enough. Crossing the room in two enormous strides, he lifted her up, her legs hoisted around his waist, stopping her with a hard kiss that pushed her head back as she groaned. His hands cradling her bottom, he stalked to the bathroom and flicked the light on, sitting her down by the sink as he continued to kiss her. He pulled back just long enough so that he could reach his hands to her top and pull it off, unfastening her bra as fast as his fingers would allow, stripping her clothing off and whipping it against the wall. He turned on the tub and it filled quickly as he took a washcloth from a small shelf on the wall. He lifted her and placed her in the tub, making short work of removing his jeans and t-shirt, aware that it was the first time the two of them had ever been completely bare to one another. He stepped into the tub, sat, and pulled her down onto his lap, straddling him.

"You've said your piece," he murmured. "And now you'll be quiet while I say mine."

She looked at him hesitantly, expectantly, and he saw hope bloom before him as he dipped the cloth in the warm water, drizzled it with her body wash she kept there, and stroked it along her back.

"You need tonight washed off of you," he whispered. "Every memory and touch gone, replaced by mine." Her eyes watched him as he washed her, first her back and then her neck, and as he draped the warm cloth over her breasts, her head fell back and she sighed.

"I love how strong you are," he whispered, as the warm water trickled over her breasts and he bent down and flicked a tongue over one hardened nipple. She hissed as he continued. "You're brilliant, and talented, and you make me so proud." He teased her second nipple with one hand as he drew the washcloth down to her legs and caressed. "I love how fearless you are. The strength in you when you choose to submit to my authority. Your bravery when you place yourself over my knee. You've put up with my shit and I'm sorry. I love you, Hillary."

She cried softly as he tilted her head back and scooped warm water over her scalp, massaging her fragrant honey-almond shampoo into her soft hair, careful to make sure the soapy water didn't get in her eyes, as he tenderly cleaned her and rinsed the lather away. "I love how sexy you are, how your body rises to meet mine when you come, and how you trust me to take care of you. I love how selfless you are to everyone around you. I love your quirky sense of humor and the cute way you wrinkle your nose." He dipped a finger between her thighs and watched as she inhaled sharply.

"I love the unreserved way you let me touch you. The way your body melts into mine when I climb into bed at night. I love the feel of your sexy little ass pressed up against my crotch." She giggled, as he continued to tease her. "I love how you eat your pizza crust first, and how you never complain when I take a sip out of your beer before I give it to you. I love that you know how to cook enchiladas, and I never told you, but I've read your books, and they're fucking awesome."

Her eyes widened and she suddenly looked up at him, panicked.

"You did not," she whispered. He chuckled.

"How else am I supposed to fulfill your fantasies, babe?"

He rinsed every bit of lather from her body, carefully touching and teasing every bit of her as he did. Standing, he lifted a large towel from the shelf, stepped out of the tub, toweled off, and cinched it around his waist. He reached for another and indicated for her to stand up. She stood, and he lifted her out of the tub, knelt in front of her and dried her while her hands rested on his shoulders. He dropped the towel and anchored himself on her bottom, kneeling in front of her while he pulled her closer and tortured her with his tongue. She moaned and he grasped her bottom to stabilize her as her hands fisted in his hair. He grinned at her, and he liked knowing she was eager for him. He stood, draping the towel over her and hoisting her into his arms.

"I love you," he whispered in her ear, as he carried her to his bedroom.

"I love you, Matteo," she said, her voice shaky and whispery.

Tomorrow he would explain himself and they would talk about how things would go from here.

Tonight, he would claim her.

Nestling her onto the bed, he stood over her, and she giggled at his obvious arousal tented under the towel.

"Is that a bump in your towel, or are you just happy to see me?" she teased.

"Brat," he half-growled, half-laughed in her ear, landing a teasing swat to her leg. She moaned. "Happy to fucking see you?" he said. "Understatement of the fucking year."

She welcomed him, opening her legs wide and arching her back, every bit of her body begging him to take her. Towels tossed to the floor, their damp bodies met and he marveled at how perfectly she fit under him, so soft and yielding. His lips met hers as he thrust into her. She was warm and as he filled her, his own heart constricted, a warmth in his belly spreading as his desire mounted.

"Jesus, baby," he groaned, and he was at a loss for words.

You feel so right.

I need this.

I don't want to let you go.

"I know," she whispered, and he saw a tear escape and roll down her cheek. "Please don't stop."

He did not. Again and again he thrust, her breath and his rising together until he came, her own climax shattering as her body trembled beneath his.

His forehead touched hers as their breathing slowed, and he braced himself so he wouldn't smother her. But he was reluctant to separate.

"I could stay like this forever," she whispered.

"Hell yeah," he groaned. "You're beautiful, and I love you."

"You're not half bad yourself," she said.

"Oh yeah?" he retorted. "For your wiseassery you shall be punished with the removal of my member."

"Ohh, oh no," she said in a half-sob half-giggle as he withdrew from her and rolled over on his side. He nabbed one of the towels and cleaned her, then pulled her up on his chest.

"Are you mine?" he whispered, running a hand down the smoothness of her naked skin, all the way to her bottom.

"All yours," she said.

"Good girl," he whispered. "We'll get some sleep now."

They'd sort out everything else in the morning. That would involve her moving in, telling Dom and Heidi, and a solid affirmation of her obedience to him, and he knew, but wouldn't tell her now lest she worry and not be able to sleep, that a nice, long, cleansing session over his knee was in order.

Those were minor details, though. What mattered most was the he was done holding himself back. She was his, and he was not going to let her go.

Chapter 11

Hillary woke slowly, keeping her eyes closed as she stretched. She could feel golden sunlight on her face, hear the sound of water running, and smell coffee brewing somewhere, but her mind was reluctant to come online. It was replaying this amazing dream where she and Matteo had made love all ni—*Oh. Wait.*

Her first clue that it hadn't been a dream came when she rolled over and the muscles of her legs and arms ached in protest. Her eyes flew open. She sat up quickly and took stock. Minor abrasions on her wrists, matching ones on her ankles, and —*oh my God*—she was definitely one hundred percent naked under these sheets... in Matteo's bed.

Her heart started beating faster and her brain finally woke up completely just as the sound of water cut off and Matteo emerged from the attached bathroom, bare chested with a towel slung around his waist. He stopped in the doorway and regarded her lounging in his bed, his expression a mixture of concern and possessive heat that made her stomach start to bubble.

"Uh... hi," she offered shyly, gripping the sheet across her chest.

His expression softened. "Hey, baby. How are you feeling?"

She contemplated for a minute and decided to go for the simplest answer.

"I'm okay, I think. A little sore," she said, displaying the faint red mark on her wrist. "And a little achy, but otherwise... okay."

He stalked closer to the bed and sat down by her hip, cupping her cheek in one strong hand.

"I'm glad you're okay physically, Tink, but I meant how are you doing mentally? Emotionally? The shit you went through last night..." He cut off and shook his head angrily, as though he'd like the opportunity to take Marauder apart again, this time more slowly and more painfully. The sight sent warmth flooding through her. "It's not the kind of thing you're just going to move on from. More than likely, shit's gonna surface from that. And when it does, *whenever* it does, you've gotta share it with me. We're a team. That's how this works."

Tears stung her eyes. "I love you," she said, biting her lip.

"I know," he told her, his smile bright, unreserved, and totally focused on her. "I love you, too."

She took a deep breath and gave him the whole truth.

"I'm really doing okay for now," she said, lifting her hand to trace a water droplet down the smooth skin of his bicep. "When I think of what happened last night, I mostly remember the way you looked when you burst into the room—like you were ready to spit fire and rip through anyone who'd hurt me. I remember the way you took care of me, at the club and... you know... *later*. And I remember that you finally told me you love me."

He narrowed his eyes, as though trying to assess whether she was telling the complete truth. She laughed softly.

"Truly, Matt," she said, moving his hand from her cheek and grasping it in both of hers. "It wasn't like last time. You were looking out for me from the beginning, you found me right away, and the whole time, I just *knew* you were coming for me. I knew I wasn't alone."

His eyes glittered into hers. "Not for a minute," he said, his voice husky.

Hillary smiled.

"So, things might come up in the future, I know you're right," she told him. "And I promise, I'll share with you, if and when it does. But for today… I think Marshall Griffson has already taken up more than enough of my time and attention. I think we need to move on, you know?"

He nodded slowly.

Another thought occurred to her and she widened her eyes in panic. "Oh, crap! Today's the rehearsal dinner! What time is it?"

She twisted her body toward the nightstand, where Matteo must have plugged her phone into charge. *Just when she thought she couldn't love him more!* She needed to call Heidi! Was Heidi freaking out?

But just as she grabbed for the phone, Matteo's hand wrapped around hers, carefully avoiding the mark on her wrist, and stopped her.

"Baby," he said, his voice low. "I get that you want to move on. And believe me, there is nothing that I'd rather do. But we have one more piece of unfinished business to discuss."

Hillary's eyes widened. "We… do?"

Hadn't everything been resolved? They were in love, and he'd rescued her like the knight in shining armor she'd known him to be.

"Last night, you eavesdropped on a conversation. *Again*," he told her gravely. "And then, far worse than that, you deliberately changed the plan, a plan that was created *specifically to ensure your safety*. And in doing so, you put yourself in jeopardy."

Hillary closed her eyes as shame washed through her. Everything that had happened last night could have been avoided if she hadn't overheard that conversation and overreacted. And, as scary as the whole experience had been for her, how terrifying had it been for Matteo? She had known with every fiber of her being that Matteo would do whatever it took, would level the freakin' city if necessary, to find her. But *he* hadn't known where she was. He hadn't known whether she was alive or dead, hurt or frightened... He hadn't known whether he'd ever see her again.

She opened her eyes.

"I'm so sorry," she told him. "I just... didn't think. I was so irresponsible."

Matteo nodded, and she could see an uncharacteristic hesitation in his face. His jaw moved back and forth, and he stared at her intently, but didn't speak.

"So... you need to punish me?" she surmised. She wasn't looking forward to it, but she knew she deserved it.

"You know what? No," he told her, standing up quickly. "You've been through enough. Let's get dressed."

Hillary frowned and grabbed for his hand as he was about to turn away.

"Wait! Matt...You've been saying that I need to tell you what I'm feeling, to be honest with you..." She shook her head. "But... I think *you* need to be honest with *me*. What happened last night didn't just happen to me... I mean, it *did*, but... it also happened to *you*. Don't you, um, need to share *your* feelings, too? Doesn't it go both ways?"

Matteo swallowed hard.

"My feelings? You wanna know *my* feelings?"

She nodded, gripping his hand more tightly.

"I've never been more scared in my entire goddamn life," he told her, removing his hand from her grasp as he turned away to stalk towards the window. She winced at the raw pain in his voice.

He laced his fingers together on top of his head, making the muscles in his back bulge and ripple.

"You know, about six years ago now, I was stationed in the sandbox. And one morning, there were five of us on this

Chinook heading for a tiny little village where insurgent activity had been reported."

She nodded encouragingly, even though he couldn't see her. She had no idea what he was talking about, but she was glad that he was talking.

"We started taking enemy fire, right? The pilot was taking evasive maneuvers, but we got hit pretty badly. One of the gunners, Reilly, was shot in the neck, he was bleeding all over the deck, the pilot was dipping and swerving so much that I legitimately thought we were gonna drop out of the sky at any point... It's happened to other guys," he said softly.

"*My God*," Hillary breathed, twisting the sheet in her lap. "What happened?"

He shrugged, as though the outcome wasn't worth discussing. "We gained altitude, the pilot was able to straighten us out and get us to base, and I held Quik-Clot to Reilly's wound until we made it back."

He turned around and looked at her, and the sunlight streaming in the window only highlighted the bleakness of his expression.

"The point is, that was the most scared I'd ever been, Tink... until last night. And back then I knew I might not make it home, but that was an acceptable risk I took to do a job I felt was worthwhile. A risk I was prepared to take. Last night? Wondering, for just a second, if maybe I'd lost you?" He shook his head. "That's not a risk I can handle."

Hillary blew out a breath. "And it was my fault," she whispered, watching him closely. "I put you through that."

He said nothing, but his jaw worked from side to side.

"You have every right to be upset at me," she told him. She shifted her weight to her knees and crawled across the bed towards him.

"I feel so stupid," she told him in a small voice. "And so, *so* sorry for worrying you and disappointing you the way I did."

"No, baby," he told her, stepping forward to grasp her face in his hands. "Stop."

"But, I did!" she cried. "Please, Matt. I need to know we're okay and that you really forgive me!"

Matt closed his eyes for a moment and shook his head ruefully. When he opened them, his bleak expression was gone.

"I was thinking that not punishing you would be the right thing to do for you," he said, sifting his fingers through the fine blonde hair at the sides of her head. "But I'm thinking *you* need it as much as I do."

What had he told her before? *Whatever the issue is, the punishment clears the air and we move on.* Would that still apply to something this huge? God, she hoped so.

"I want us to be right again," she whispered, gazing up at him.

"We will be," he told her firmly, his clear green eyes meeting hers. A little knot of tension she hadn't known she'd been carrying loosened.

"Hillary, do you know why I'm angry with you?" he asked solemnly.

She wet her suddenly dry lips. "Because I eavesdropped on your conversation... *again*," she said in a soft voice. "Because I disobeyed and put myself in danger."

He nodded. "Those things, yes. But because, above everything, there needs to be trust between us. You need to trust me in order to obey me. And I need to trust that you *will* obey me and keep yourself safe."

Hillary nodded, tears of remorse stinging her eyes.

"Present yourself for punishment, baby."

Hillary bit her lip. Her breath hitched as she turned herself around on her knees. As she lowered her chest and felt the slick coolness of the sheets against her nipples, her heart began to beat in a crazy rhythm. She dreaded this as much as she craved it.

How was it possible to both want something and dread it *simultaneously?*

She pressed her cheek to the mattress, stretched her arms out in front of her, and heard Matteo inhale sharply behind her.

"That's right, Hillary. Arch for me. Just like that," he told her. "Don't move." His tone was stern and demanding, but there was a raspy catch in his voice that promised pleasure. She shivered and closed her eyes.

She could hear him moving behind her, and she was curious, but didn't dare lift her head to look around. Minutes passed. The HVAC system had kicked on, and the soft breeze on her backside made her break out in goose bumps, as every nerve in her body tensed in anticipation, but she was resolved to stay in position as long as it took. She wouldn't fail him again.

A moment later, he was behind her once more, and his warm, callused hand roved over the curve of her backside. "That's my good girl," he told her, and Hillary felt tears spring to her eyes. It was exactly what she'd needed to hear.

"I'm going to use the hairbrush on you, Hillary," he told her. Her breath caught. He'd never used that on her before. *Crap.*

"Should you have been eavesdropping on me, Hillary? Didn't you learn your lesson about honesty last time?" he asked. A wave of shame rushed up from her belly, catching her unawares. She tamped it down ruthlessly.

"No, sir," she whispered.

Thwack! Bright sparks of pain blossomed across her skin and Hillary bit her lip. It wasn't *so* awful. She deserved it, and she could take it.

Thwack, thwack, thwack, thwack. Four more strokes fell across her ass in quick succession, and her entire backside tingled hotly.

"You disobeyed me, Hillary," he told her.

"Yes, sir," she agreed.

Several more hard lashes rained down, until her entire

awareness had become centered on her backside, on each burst of pain melding into the whole.

"You. Are. Mine," he told her.

Then three more strokes landed nearly on top of one another, all clustered lower down, near her thighs. Tears sprang to her eyes and she blinked them back furiously.

"And when you risk yourself," he continued, "by disobeying me, by failing to trust me, you are risking the most precious thing *in my universe*."

Thwack, thwack, thwack.

On and on it seemed to go, to the point where Hillary lost count. Surely he would be done soon? Each fresh tongue of fire proved her wrong.

She'd been determined to hold onto her composure, to accept her punishment meekly, but as the stinging strokes continued to fall, she felt herself begin to squirm. Matteo's firm hand at her back pushed her back down.

"Hold your position!" he told her, with another firm blow to her sit spot.

Shit!

This was way longer than any spanking he'd ever given her. What was he thinking?

"Matteo, please, are we done?" she begged, in what she hoped was a meek voice.

"You'll be done when I say you're done, Hillary," he told her, his voice not angry but determined.

"But I can't take any more!" she cried.

"Your safeword is *red*, Hillary, remember?" he said briskly.

Thwack, thwack, thwack.

Shit. Did she need to safeword? The spanking was beyond painful, yes, but it wasn't truly more than she could handle. She just wanted to know how much more to expect so that she could brace for it, so that she could... control it.

Oh.

And Matteo knew that. Because Matteo knew her.

And he loved her. And he knew what she could handle.

She *could* trust him. She *had* to trust him. She had to let go.

The realization brought tears to her eyes that she couldn't keep back and no longer wanted to. A sob welled up from deep in her chest, and before she knew it, she was crying—full on bawling, in a way that she hadn't allowed herself to cry in years.

And Matteo was there through it all. He stopped spanking her and instead began stroking her hair, telling her he loved her, rubbing her back, and reminding her that she was his good girl and he would never, *never* let her go.

By the time her tears stopped and the emotional tsunami receded, Hillary felt lighter. Buoyant. Cleansed. *Whole*. And blissfully in love. She'd never met someone who could make her feel so many things at once... and who embraced her emotions so completely.

Just when she thought she couldn't handle another emotion, Matteo stroked his hands up her thighs, readying her, sending bright ripples of sensation straight to her core... and she found she could handle just a little more.

"God, I've dreamed about this," he groaned, his hands holding her hips firmly. "About you yielding to me the way you did, about sliding inside you this way."

His words, the picture they conjured, made her ache, even as he filled her.

"Is it as good as you dreamed it would be?" she asked breathlessly.

He rocked his hips against her backside and made her gasp from the blissful combination of pleasure and pain. Nothing had ever felt so totally *right*, so perfect.

"Shit, baby," he panted. "If I'd had a dream like *this*, I never would've woken up."

And then, against all probability, Hillary found herself snorting with laughter even as her cheeks were still wet from her tears. Because apparently there was no limit to how many emotions she'd feel when she was with Matteo. And that was fine with her.

Matteo grabbed her hand and dragged her, giggling, down the street to *Cara*, her high heels slapping loudly on the pavement as they ran.

"We are so fucking late for this rehearsal," he growled at her unnecessarily.

Hillary had already received three progressively more impatient calls from Heidi, wondering where Hillary was, and she knew Matt had received at least one call from Dom. She was probably shirking her duty as bridesmaid, but Hillary couldn't bring herself to care as much as she should. Marauder was in jail, all of their friends and family were safe and happy (if somewhat annoyed), and Matteo was holding her hand. Everything beyond that was just details.

"You were the one who insisted on making sure I couldn't remember what Slay's kiss had felt like," she reminded him helpfully, pressing her swollen lips together at the memory. He'd been exceptionally thorough.

He stopped short just in front of the entrance, causing Hillary to knock into him from behind, and looked back over his shoulder at her.

"And you were the one who kept reminding me that you have an excellent memory," he told her, his gorgeous green eyes twinkling.

"That's true," she admitted, smiling at him. "But I didn't expect you to have to take me back to bed to make 'extra sure'."

He turned around to face her more fully and wrapped his arms around her waist, the heat of him sinking through the thin material of her frilly dress and light sweater. "Babe, if there's an opportunity for me to take you to bed, you can pretty much expect I'm going to take it."

Hillary laughed, and set her hands on his shoulders, which looked broader than ever in his gray suit jacket. "So you're saying I just have to give you an opportunity?" she challenged.

His eyes narrowed. "Behave yourself," he told her, squeezing her ass just enough to remind her of the punishment she'd received earlier in the day. "And I'll find my own opportunity… later."

Hillary squirmed. "Yes, sir," she whispered. "I'm going to be a perfect angel."

He rolled his eyes as he grabbed the door handle and ushered her inside. "This I've gotta see."

Then they were inside the dark lobby, and Hillary couldn't reply, at least not in a meaningful way.

She and Matt had discussed it, and decided that they wouldn't go public with their relationship just yet. They were committed to one another, no doubt, but they were bound to raise a few eyebrows at first, and they didn't want to cause any more drama before Heidi and Dom's wedding. It had seemed simple enough, but as Matt took a careful step away from her, she had to fight her instinct to close the distance and touch him again. She could tell from his scowl that Matt felt the same way.

"Sooner we get in there, the sooner we'll be done," he whispered.

Hillary nodded.

But before she could take a step towards the dining room where the wedding was to be held, Tessa ran out, sobbing, crashing into Hillary and almost knocking her over.

"Oh, God, I'm so sorry, Hillie," Tess said. "I just need to…" She lifted a hand towards the ladies' room, which was located off the lobby.

"Tess, what happened?" Hillary asked, sliding an arm around the other woman's waist.

Tess shook her head and ran toward the bathroom, just as a very pissed-off Tony and a very soggy-looking Valerie emerged from the dining room.

"This is absolutely the last straw, Tony!" Val screeched. "Just look at what that bitch did! Red wine will *never* come out! And this dress is *Balenciaga!*"

The front of Val's hair was clinging to her face in wet clumps, her tight, white strapless dress was liberally splashed with purple, and Val seemed to have trouble standing upright in her shoes.

Hillary bit her lip to keep from giggling, but Matteo didn't bother—he snorted outright.

Tony rounded on Val, shaking his head. "Well, maybe if you hadn't accused her of trying to seduce me in front of the whole party, she wouldn't have! Jesus, Valerie." Beneath the deep current of anger in his voice, there was exhaustion and resignation.

Turning to Matteo and Hillary, he asked, "Did you see where Tess went? I need to talk to her and sort this out."

"Um... ladies' room," Hillary said quietly.

Tony looked at the ladies' room door hesitantly for a moment, as though he was contemplating barging inside, but thought better of it. He ran a hand through his hair and sighed.

"You guys are late," he said, looking back and forth between them, a frown on his face.

But Val didn't want to be ignored. Before Matt or Hillary could say a word, Val stepped in front of Tony and crossed her arms over her chest. "You don't see what I see, Tony. That woman has been after you from the moment she darkened your door, and you're blind to it! You treat her like she's the second coming, for God's sake. 'Tessa says *this*' and 'Tess told me *that*'. Well, what about *me*, Tony?"

Tony sighed wearily. "What *about* you, Val?"

Valerie's eyes sparked fire. "*I* try to give you advice! *I* try to offer you my encouragement! But you don't want it. You'd rather spend your time with that... that... Do you even *know* what she's like, Tony? Do you *know* what she likes to do with her spare time?"

Beside Hillary, Matteo stiffened. She glanced quickly at his face to find that his eyes had narrowed on Valerie.

"I really don't *care* what she does in her spare time, Val. She's a good person. And she's a damn good manager," Tony said hotly.

But Val continued as though he hadn't spoken, a sickening air of triumph in her voice. "She goes to a club for *sexual deviants!* One of the girls from my salon saw her there. She likes to be tied up and beaten and *who knows what*! That the kind of woman you want, Tony?"

Tony gaped at Valerie dumbly, his mouth hanging open, and Hillary felt her own face mirror his. Was Tessa a submissive?

Matteo stepped forward and put his hand on Valerie's elbow.

"*Enough*," he said firmly. "Tess is a friend of mine. It's time for you to go."

"Fuck you!" Val said, ripping her elbow from his grasp. "This is Tony's restaurant, not yours!"

Hillary could see that Val was unsteady on her feet, and wondered how much wine Val had consumed before Tessa had finally snapped.

Matteo looked at Tony, expecting him to take charge of the situation, but Tony was still staring at Val in shock.

"Are you one of them?" Val asked Matteo, her voice slurred.

"I don't even want to know what you're talking about," Matteo said coldly. "It's definitely time for you to—"

"You *are!* You're one of those sick bastards!" Val accused, cradling her elbow as though Matteo had injured her. "You get off on abusing women!"

"Tony, for Christ's sake, get her out of here!" Matteo barked, frustrated when Tony *still* didn't seem to hear him.

Hillary understood his frustration. Val was causing a scene, but Matteo would no more physically restrain Valerie against her will than he would fly—it went against everything he believed in.

But it suddenly occurred to Hillary that she had no such constraints.

She stepped forward and pushed Val firmly in the chest, knocking the other woman back a step.

"You shut your filthy mouth!" Hillary hissed. "You don't have the first idea what you're talking about. Matteo doesn't abuse women—if he did, your ass would be out in the middle of the street right now."

"Hillary," Matteo said in a warning tone, wrapping his arm around her waist from behind. But Hillary ignored him. It was stupid stuff like what Val was spouting that made women afraid to ask for what they wanted from men, afraid they'd be called deviants, or *worse*. And it was that fear, that need to hide, that made them easy prey for the truly perverted people, like Marauder.

"Your ignorance is appalling," Hillary continued. "Dominance is not about abuse. Submission isn't about liking to be beaten. It's about freedom and trust and unconditional *love*. It's beautiful! There is *nothing* wrong with that. What you do to Tony, on the other hand, is fucking abusive! You use him for his money, you don't care about what he wants, and you try to bully him—"

"Enough," Matt growled in her ear. "Tink! You have an audience."

Hillary's gaze flew up to see Heidi, Dom, Paul, John, and... *oh, crap*!... her parents, standing in the doorway to the dining room. Every eye was trained on her as she stood in Matteo's arms, defending submission at the top of her lungs.

So much for keeping things low key until after the wedding. Great job avoiding drama, Hillary.

Her parents looked confused. Heidi was biting her lip anxiously. Paul looked amused. His boyfriend, John, winked at

Hillary and clapped silently. And Dom... *oh, Lord*. Dom looked like he was about to have a stroke.

Just then, someone in the dining room cleared his throat loudly, and the crowd in the doorway parted to show the baffled-looking minister.

"Mr. Angelico? Miss Morrow?" he asked impatiently. "Are you ready to begin?"

Heidi turned to beam at the man, a manic gleam in her eyes. "Yes, sir! Everyone's here, so we'll be ready to begin, uh... in one minute."

The minister nodded and stepped back into the dining room.

"Mom, Dad—um, could you please wait with Dr. Epping?" Heidi begged. And when it seemed like their mother was about to protest, she interjected, "Tell him about your new African water charity! I'm sure he'd be thrilled." Frances's eyes lit up and she scurried off after the man.

"And Paul, why don't you, um, escort Valerie to her car?" Heidi said, her tone hardening.

Paul nodded, but before he could step forward, Tony snapped out of his reverie and held up a hand.

"That won't be necessary," he told Paul. Then, turning back to Val, he said, "You've had too much to drink. You can't drive. I'm calling you a cab."

Valerie's face turned white, then quickly flushed a deep purple.

"No fucking way," she whispered harshly. "Didn't you hear the way she talked to me, Tony? Did you see the way he grabbed me? It's completely unacceptable! If you kick me out, I'll... I'll..."

Tony looked at her as though he'd never seen her before. "You'll what? Never forgive me? Fine. Trash me to your friends? I'm used to it. Frankly, Val, I just don't give a shit anymore."

Val's eyes widened with shock and hurt. "You'd better take a minute to think about what you're saying!" she cried. "Because if you tell me to go, if you choose *them* over *me*, I'm never coming back."

Tony rubbed his hand over his eyes.

"Fine," he said, sighing. "Fine. Val, you've been giving me ultimatums from the beginning. It's like some kind of game with you—*testing* me, waiting to see if I'm going to pick you, like you've been waiting for me to fail you." He shook his head sadly. "I swear, I thought if I just picked you often enough… But I realize now that it'll never be enough, will it? There will always be another test. I will never make you happy."

As Val watched in horror, Tony strode over to the reception desk, picked up the phone, and hit a number on speed-dial.

"I'm calling from *Cara* on Hanover Street," he said into the receiver. "I need a cab." Then he looked at Val. "Grab your purse. I'll wait with you outside."

"Don't bother," Val spat, and she stomped out the door. Tony stood by the window and watched her go.

A strained silence followed her departure. John mumbled something to Paul, and then made his way to the ladies' room. Checking on Tessa.

Hillary shook her head. *Damn.* She'd honestly hoped to see Tony end things a long time ago, but *gosh*… not like this. And she felt more than a little responsible for the way things had escalated.

Hillary darted a look at Matteo. She knew she'd be in trouble for losing her temper at Val the way she had, but she wasn't sure exactly *how* mad he'd be…

But Matteo wasn't looking at her. His arm was still locked around her waist, but he was staring across the lobby at Dom, who looked ready to commit murder.

Damn, again.

Heidi touched Dom's arm. "Dom, honey, please? Dr. Epping is waiting for us. We can discuss all this later."

Dom nodded, then his eyes flicked down to Heidi, and

narrowed. "You don't seem very surprised about seeing your sister with my brother, Heidi," he said.

Heidi flushed and stammered, and Hillary mentally rolled her eyes. Could Heidi possibly look any guiltier?

"Dom, I, um… Well, I had *suspicions*…"

Dom raised an eyebrow and looked at Heidi with a kind of reined-in anger that reminded Hillary of Matteo.

"We'll discuss this later, Heidi," he told her, and Heidi nodded meekly. Hillary shivered in sympathy. Heidi would be getting punished.

Matteo put his hand on Hillary's back and led her toward the dining room.

"And you and I will have a discussion later, too, Matteo," Dom said in a low voice, as they came close.

Matteo raised his chin. "You wanna talk, we'll talk, Dom. But I'm telling you now, it's not going to change anything."

Dom inhaled sharply. "You promised me…"

Matteo nodded. "I did. And I shouldn't have. I knew even then that this was different, that *Hillary* was different."

Dom narrowed his eyes skeptically and opened his mouth to retort, but Tony came up behind them looking haggard and tired.

"Guys, I think the minister's waiting," he told them firmly, stepping between them. "It's your fucking wedding rehearsal, Dom!" he said with uncharacteristic aggression, when it seemed like Dom would speak.

Dom inhaled sharply and looked away from Matteo. "Ready, baby?" he asked Heidi.

Heidi nodded. "So ready," she told him.

And together they made their way toward the minister, where he waited under the flower-draped arch on the far side of the room.

The rehearsal passed quickly and uneventfully, after its disastrous start. Dom and Heidi, flanked by Matteo and Hillary,

His Submissive

walked through their entrances and exits. Heidi's happiness and excitement were palpable, and seemed to diffuse some of Dom's anger... though not all of it. At one point, Hillary noticed Dom looking at Matteo stonily as Matteo took Hillary's arm to lead her up the aisle.

"Maybe if I talked to him?" Hillary offered Matteo in a whisper. "I appreciate that he's being all protective and brotherly. But maybe if I explained that he doesn't need to be?"

Matteo shook his head firmly. "Nah. Dom knows that. Or if he doesn't, he'll figure it out. Don't worry, baby. It's gonna be fine."

Hillary wasn't so sure, but she nodded. She trusted that Matteo would find a way to make it so.

Immediately after the rehearsal, Tony ushered everyone into the function room off the dining room, where a single long table had been set up. She was seated near her mother and Matteo on one end of the table, while Dom, Heidi, and her father were at the other end, and Paul, John, Tony, and Tess, who had been dragged from the ladies' room and cajoled into attending, formed a buffer in the middle.

John and Paul were as charming as she'd ever seen them, and her parents were, thank God, on their best behavior, but the tension around the table was still thick. Tess ate nothing and barely spoke, Tony was watchful, Matteo's quick humor was missing, Dom was even quieter than usual, and Hillary's sore backside had been aching since the moment she sat down. Finally, as the wait staff cleared away the plates of chicken picatta and prepared to serve dessert, Tony stood up and cleared his throat.

"So, um... Usually the best man or the father of the bride is supposed to give a toast at the rehearsal dinner," he said, glancing around at all of them. "But hopefully Matt and Charles don't mind if I butt in first?"

Matteo shook his head, and so did Hillary's father.

Tony nodded and cleared his throat again.

"I'm sitting here thinking about family—both the family we're born into," he looked at Dom and Matt, "and the family we choose," he said, nodding at Paul and John and Tess. "You all know that Dom and Matt and I come from this big Italian family. You've met most of them and Lord knows you'll meet *all* of them tomorrow…"

"God help us all," Matteo muttered, and everyone, including Tony, chuckled.

"Exactly. But it just kind of occurred to me that there are some people missing from our table tonight. Some people who *should* be here, but can't be. Our mom. Our dad. Our Nana Angelico."

The table fell silent, everyone staring at Tony.

"My mom would've loved you, Heidi," he told her, his voice ringing with emotion. "She would've loved your big heart, your generosity, your strength, and the way you work hard to take care of everyone you love. My Nana, well… she would've loved the way you love Dom. The way he loves you."

Heidi smiled and bit her lip.

"And it sucks that you'll never get to know her. So I, um… thought I'd tell you guys a story."

He cleared his throat once more.

"There's this legend in our family," he began. "That our Nana Angelico used to be known as a witch."

Dom snorted and Hillary saw Matteo roll his eyes.

Tony chuckled. "Right, well, she wasn't *really* a witch, *obviously*, but she was a hell of an entrepreneur. Back when she was a young widow in Italy, raising my dad and all his sisters, she made a living for their family by casting 'love spells' for all the girls in the village."

"No. Way!" Hillary said. She looked at Matt for confirmation, and he nodded reluctantly. *How cool was that?*

Tony laughed again.

"Seriously. At first, young girls would come to her saying, 'I can't get this guy to like me,' and she'd give the girl advice, help her find true love. And she got so *good* at it, that people would come from other villages—not just teenage girls coming for advice, but their *parents* coming, ready to pay big bucks to get their girls a good husband."

"And it worked?" Heidi asked incredulously.

Tony smiled. "Every time. She was famous for being a matchmaker."

"So, what happened?" Hillary's dad asked. "You said she *used to be* known as a witch."

Tony nodded. "One day, after my dad was grown and his sisters were all married off—to loving, eligible men, of course—this girl and her parents came to visit my Nana. Now, most of Nana's business had dried up by this time. We're talking 1970-something, right? Girls were thinking of college or careers in the city, not getting married to some guy from the next village. But this girl's parents were *extremely* wealthy. And their only daughter, Teresa, who was just nineteen, was known far and wide for her beauty. They were already inundated with offers from various guys. But they didn't want a *good* match for her. They wanted an *excellent* match. They wanted a *perfect* match. And they had a really good idea of what that would entail, of course. Someone rich, of course. Someone good looking…"

"Don't wanna take a chance on ugly grandkids," John said, and everyone snickered.

"Right! And you know, as a secondary consideration, maybe someone with more brains than a potato who wasn't a serial killer," Tony continued.

Hillary's mother gasped in outrage. "That poor girl!"

Tony nodded. "That's what my Nana thought. And the more she talked with the girl, the more sympathetic she became. The girl didn't want a rich man, or a distinguished man, she wanted a *loving* man. Someone she could *trust*."

"So… what did she do?" Hillary asked softly, leaning closer to Matteo.

"Nana sent the girl to the village market to buy bread," he said, his eyes dancing.

Hillary and Heidi exchanged amused glances.

"Bread?" Tess asked, the first word she'd spoken since they sat down.

"Mm-hmm. And then Nana took the girl's parents into her living room to negotiate terms. She promised them that the girl would find her dream man, and be married by the end of the week."

"And was she?" Tess demanded.

"You know it." Tony nodded then smiled, first at Matteo and then at Dom. "You see, our dad worked in the bakery. And Nana knew her son. She knew if he took one *look* at Teresa, he'd need to *talk* to her, and that if he spent one minute *talking* to her, he'd get down on his knees and *propose*. And yeah," he said to Tess, who had opened her mouth to interrupt. "That's exactly how it happened."

"My Nana was *not* a witch," he continued, looking up and down the table. "But she was a *really* smart lady. She knew that people could sometimes be blind to the most obvious things, and have grand and misguided ideas and expectations about what's *proper* and *best*—for themselves and everyone around them. But she also knew that if you put the *right* two people in a room, they would orient themselves to one another… the way a compass always finds true north." He looked at Hillary… and then at Dom. "Because that's how true love works."

Dom looked away and frowned.

"What happened with her parents?" Heidi asked, enthralled in the story.

Tony smiled. "Well… you might notice I haven't mentioned my Nana or Papa Puliafico?" he said, and Heidi burst out laughing. "It's because I've never met them. My mom's parents were pissed. My dad wasn't rich or even well educated. And, uh... frankly, he had a hell of a reputation with the ladies," Tony admitted, scratching his head and giving Matteo a wry look. "They disowned her."

"That's terrible! It should've been *her* choice!" Heidi said.

"Yeah," Tony agreed. "But, you know, in their defense, they were really worried. They *genuinely* believed that a certain type of guy would make her happy."

"Ridiculous!" Hillary exclaimed. "She knew her own mind!"

Tony nodded and looked at Dom once more.

"Yeah," he said softly. "She did."

Dom pursed his lips and said nothing.

"So," Tony continued, "that was where it all started. They came to Boston, because my Aunt Lina lived here with her husband. They had two *practice* children, before finally having *me* a few years later..."

"Accidentally!" Dom and Matteo interrupted at the same time, then looked at each other and smiled as the table erupted in laughter.

"You mean *unexpectedly*," Tony corrected them with a grin. "Like a *blessing from Heaven*, as Mom used to say..."

Matteo rolled his eyes.

"Now, my dad was this *big* guy. Bigger than Matteo," he said, gesturing to Matt with one hand. "And my mom, she was even smaller than Hillary."

"Is that possible?" Paul asked, winking at her across the table.

Hillary narrowed her eyes and stuck out her tongue, before Matteo put a hand on her chair and hauled her closer to him.

"And my dad was the loud one of the two of them—the man had an opinion about *everything* and didn't hesitate to share it... I'm trying to think which of us inherited that trait," he said, glancing at Dom, who scowled while Matteo chuckled.

"But anyone who knew them knew that my mom was the *heart* of our family, and that my dad thought the sun rose and set for her. We come from a line of really strong women," he said softly, looking around the table. "And, fortunately for you, Heidi, from a line of men who are smart enough to pick strong women and do whatever it takes, *whatever it takes*, to keep them happy."

When Tony looked at Dom this time, Dom nodded. Then he slowly turned his head and nodded at Matteo and Hillary. He understood and he approved. Beside her, Hillary felt Matteo's chin lift, and felt his body relax. Hillary moved closer to his side, relief and gladness making her dizzy.

"You all know that my Dad died back when I was in high school," Tony continued, and she saw him pause and take a deep breath before continuing. "My mom... she was devastated. But she was never bitter, not for one minute. Because she knew how lucky she was to have *had* him, how lucky they were to have found each other. She told me... ah..." He swallowed hard before continuing. "She told me she was grateful for every day she'd gotten to wake up beside him. And that's always stuck with me, you know?"

He looked up and down the table once more.

"Relationships are not easy," he said. "There will always be give and take. And there will be times when you mess up and let each other down." His gaze found Tess, who stared back at him intently. "When you try to do the right thing, and fail. But I think, maybe, as long as you're *committed*, as long as you're willing to pick up where you are and try again, as long as you can wake up every day next to the person you love and feel *grateful*, then you've got... well... everything."

"So... I propose a toast," he continued, and everyone obligingly raised their glasses. "To Dom and Heidi... who have *each other*, and so... have *everything*."

Dom and Heidi looked at one another. Hillary saw tears fall down her sister's cheeks, and Dom brushed them off with his thumb before he leaned in and kissed her tenderly.

God, Hillary thought, sniffling. She was ready to cry already, and it was only the freakin' *rehearsal dinner*. What kind of a mess would she be at the wedding?

As the other guests broke off and began talking amongst themselves, Matteo leaned over and whispered in her ear. "Tears, Tink? I can't say I blame you."

Hillary leaned her head against his. "It's just so beautiful, you know? I can't help it. Seeing Heidi so happy. Knowing that Dom is okay with us being together. I'm kind of a mess." She gave a watery laugh.

"Ohhh," Matt said, wrapping his arm around her waist. "Is *that* what you're crying over?"

She turned to look at him. "Of course! What else would it be?"

Matt answered in a low voice. "Well, if I were sitting on a bottom as sore as yours must be after this morning…"

Hillary squirmed. It seemed to ache even more now that he mentioned it.

"And if I'd earned myself as serious a punishment as you did tonight…" Matt shrugged. "I might succumb to a few tears, too."

Oh. Oh, *shit*.

Matteo looked at her face and chuckled, the rat.

"Ah, poor Tink! So much for being a 'perfect angel', hmm?" He tucked a strand of hair behind her ear and smiled.

Hillary sighed and leaned into his hand. "Yeah, that… may have been aiming a bit high, in retrospect."

He laughed again. "That's okay, baby. I've never had a thing for angels anyway."

"No?" That was fortunate, given her track record.

"Nah. I prefer women who are smart and strong and sassy. When a capable, resilient woman chooses to submit, baby, that's a priceless gift."

"You think *I* am all those things?" she asked in surprise.

"Of course. You're my Tinker Bell. Feisty, fearless, loyal…"

He leaned closer to whisper in her ear and make her shiver. "Cute as hell."

"So… all this time that I've been hating that stupid name… it was a *compliment*? Gosh, Matt, I totally misjudged you," she said, smiling and shaking her head. "I thought it was just because I was, you know… short."

"Well, yeah! I mean, *that's* definitely true, too," he agreed, his eyes glinting when he saw her outraged expression.

Hillary's eyes narrowed. He liked her feisty? *Good.*

A waitress put a plate of gooey chocolate cake in front of each guest, and Hillary waited until Matt had taken a large bite before leaning over and asking casually, "So, is, um… *Slay* coming tonight?"

Matteo choked on his cake and turned to glare at her. "No. Why would he? He's not in the wedding party."

Hillary adopted her most innocent expression… Heidi could *totally* learn from her example.

"Oh, right! Of course. *Duh!*" she said brightly, and applied herself to savoring the chocolate cake. She pretended not to notice that Matt had stopped eating and was looking at her with a frown on his face.

"Mmm," she said. "Wow. This cake is so—"

"Why did you ask about Slay?" Matteo interrupted.

"Pardon? Oh," Hillary said, licking the back of her spoon dreamily. "Well, it's just that memory is a funny thing, isn't it?"

Matteo's eyes flared. "Are you remembering him kissing you?" he demanded.

Gotcha, Hillary thought.

She widened her eyes dramatically. "What! *No*! I mean, not on *purpose*, Matt. I just can't help it!"

"Oh, you can help it," he growled, and she could barely suppress her instinctive shiver. "Stop it this instant."

She shrugged helplessly and toyed with her spoon. "It's just that when he kissed me, I…"

"What?" he demanded, taking the spoon from her fingers and forcing her to look at him.

"I felt, um..." she faltered.

"What?" he insisted. "What did you feel with *him* that you don't feel with *me*?"

"I felt so very..." She lifted her eyes to his. "Tall," she deadpanned.

"Tall?" he repeated blankly.

Hillary saw his face change the instant he realized what she'd done, and she couldn't hold back her giggle. She grabbed her spoon and took another bite of chocolate cake.

"Oh, Tinker Bell," he said sadly, leaning back to fold his arms across his chest. "Enjoy your time in that chair, baby. Pretty sure you'll be standing all day tomorrow."

She winked at him. "Worth it!" she said saucily.

"'Though she be but little, she is fierce,'" he quoted, shaking his head. "Shakespeare could've been talking about my girl when he wrote that." He reached over and tugged on a strand of her hair. "Love you, baby."

Hillary looked down at the table and smiled to herself. Was she fierce and strong and all those other things he'd called her? She didn't know, and it didn't matter. She was loved. And she was *his*.

Epilogue

The sun shone brightly the next day, the day of Dom and Heidi's wedding. It was a gorgeous fall day in New England. Sunny and warm, the leaves on the large oaks and maples rustling in the breeze, fully emblazoned with colors of rust, auburn, gold and crimson so picturesque, guests were busily snapping photos of the front lawn of the church even before the limo arrived with the girls. But when it did arrive, and the bridesmaids and bride stepped out of the limo, Matteo only had eyes for one.

Her eyes found his immediately, and warmed. It seemed so long ago that he'd first laid eyes on the dress she wore now. They'd come so far. She was wearing the soft, shimmery, strapless dress the color of spun gold, with a silky brown band around her waist, and gold heeled sandals that were so damn sexy he'd taken her right over his lap the night before wearing nothing but those. The memory made him shift with arousal. God, what that girl did to him. She was even more gorgeous than she'd been when he'd first laid eyes on her in that dress, and now he knew why. He felt a pang in his chest, a stab of joy. She was more lovely than ever because now she was his.

His eyes trailed over her body, down to her ankles, and he remembered how he'd held her in bed and softly massaged the red marks from her wrists and ankles, after a night of dark, passionate, erotic pleasure. He was getting hard just looking at her. He was a total goner.

"Jesus, man, wipe the drool from your mouth, will ya?" muttered Slay's deep voice in Matteo's ear.

"Oh shut the fuck up," Matteo hissed, ignoring Slay's teasing chuckle.

"You're fucking incorrigible," Slay countered.

"Will you two behave yourselves," chided a female voice to Matteo's left, and Matteo looked up to see Alice holding onto Slay's arm, standing a good head below him, shaking her head while her eyes twinkled.

"Hey, Alice," Matteo greeted with a nod, as Hillary turned with the group of girls and scooped up Heidi's train, flicking it so that it fell gracefully as they entered the quaint church. Matteo caught Hillary's eye and gave her a raucous wink. She nearly tripped, and he shook his head at her as she gave him a sheepish look. Good to know he could affect her like that, even from a distance.

He'd tied her up and had his way with her until she screamed in ecstasy. He'd spanked her, not as punishment but a deliciously slow spanking that heightened her senses and turned him on, until she fairly begged for him to allow her to climax. They'd sat in bed and watched chick flicks—not his thing, but he was happy to oblige her, happy just to eat the popcorn and have her lying next to him. He'd tucked her in when she was ready to sleep, whispering to her how much he loved her and how beautiful she was to him.

Beautiful. Lovely. And next week, when Dom and Heidi were on their honeymoon, she would sit atop the chair in his studio and he would give her a new tattoo. He'd tried to talk her into getting a Tinker Bell tat, but she'd only smacked his arm and poked him, which landed her belly-down over his lap and screaming with laughter as he smacked her cute little ass. Instead, he'd ink the words they'd chosen in script on her shoulder. A tat had never held so much meaning for him.

Though she be but little, she is fierce.

Fierce. Fiercely loyal. Fiercely strong. Fiercely loving.

They entered the church and Matteo went to Dom, giving him a quick pep talk, and Dom was pumped. They'd waited a long time for this day, and now the day had come.

"You're almost there. Heidi's beautiful, man," Matteo muttered to Dom, giving him a fist bump right before they took their places in the church. And she was. But as the organ played and a hush fell over the church, Matteo watched as Hillary began the walk down the aisle, a cluster of white and red roses held close, but her eyes trained on him. He smiled, and she smiled back, her face lighting up, radiant and lovely. She was his.

His friend.
His girl.
His lover.
His submissive.

The End

Jane Henry

USA Today bestselling author Jane Henry pens stern but loving alpha heroes, feisty heroines, and emotion-driven happily-ever-afters. She writes what she loves to read: kink with a tender touch. Jane is a hopeless romantic who lives on the East Coast with a houseful of children and her very own Prince Charming.

Don't miss these exciting titles by Jane Henry and Blushing Books!

A Thousand Yesses

Bound to You series
Begin Again, Book 1
Come Back To Me, Book 2
Complete Me, Book 3

Boston Doms Series
By Jane Henry and Maisy Archer
My Dom, Book 1
His Submissive, Book 2
Her Protector, Book 3
His Babygirl, Book 4
His Lady, Book 5
Her Hero, Book 6
My Redemption, Book 7

Anthologies

Hero Undercover
Sunstrokes

Connect with Jane Henry
janehenrywriter.blogspot.com
janehenrywriter@gmail.com

Blushing Books

Blushing Books is one of the oldest eBook publishers on the web. We've been running websites that publish spanking and BDSM related romance and erotica since 1999, and we have been selling eBooks since 2003. We hope you'll check out our hundreds of offerings at http://www.blushingbooks.com.

CPSIA information can be obtained
at www.ICGtesting.com
Printed in the USA
LVHW011636180520
655945LV00004B/444